What Bad Bitches Do 3

Aryanna

Lock Down Publications and
Ca$h Presents

What Bad Bitches Do 3

A Novel by Aryanna

Aryanna

Lock Down Publications

P.O. Box 870494
Mesquite, Tx 75187

Visit our website
www.lockdownpublications.com

Lock Down Publications
Like our page on Facebook: Lock Down Publications @
www.facebook.com/lockdownpublications.ldp
Cover design and layout by: **Dynasty Cover Me**
Book interior design by: **Shawn Walker**
Edited by: **Jill Alicea**

Stay Connected with Us!

Text **LOCKDOWN** to 22828 to stay up-to-date with new releases, sneak peeks, contests and more…

Submission Guideline.

Submit the first three chapters of your completed manuscript to ldpsubmissions@gmail.com, subject line: Your book's title. The manuscript must be in a .doc file and sent as an attachment. The document should be in Times New Roman, double-spaced and in size 12 font. Also, provide your synopsis and full contact information. If sending multiple submissions, they must each be in a separate email.

Have a story but no way to send it electronically? You can still submit to LDP/Ca$h Presents. Send in the first three chapters, written or typed, of your completed manuscript to:

LDP: Submissions Dept
Po Box 870494
Mesquite, Tx 75187

DO NOT send original manuscript. Must be a duplicate.

Provide your synopsis and a cover letter containing your full contact information.

Thanks for considering LDP and Ca$h Presents.

Dedication:

This book is dedicated to every bad bitch that ain't afraid to own it.

Acknowledgements:

God, I thank you for the continued blessings as well as the struggles along the way because they both serve to humble and motivate me. I have to thank my significant other, best friend, soulmate, and other half. Our love has flourished under distance, trials, tribulations, outside interference, as well as circumstances beyond our control, but I wouldn't change it because its proven to be the definition of real. I love you babe! I have to thank my kids (the next generation) for your love and support, and for being the reason I smile. I love you beyond words. I have to thank my family for still allowing me to turn to you even though I'm grown. I'll never be too old to need a hug. I absolutely have to thank my fans and supporters because I couldn't do this without you! trust me I'll never forget that you helped make me, and I love all of you. I have to thank my LDP family for rocking with me and motivating me to make my next book better than my last one. I got you. I have to thank every single person who is stuck behind the g-wall and finds themselves caught up in the page of one of my stories. I appreciate you allowing me to entertain you. I have to thank my haters for still being here for me. Lol! Shout out to my nigga General Monk! I ain't forgot you comrade, and our collaboration is a must! Shout out all the real muthafucka in my life, and since you know who you are I know I ain't gotta say your name. Thank you for everything!

Aryanna

Chapter 1
Ebony
Aruba

"Here you go, Miss, a non-alcoholic banana daiquiri."

"Thank you," I replied, pointing to a spot where he could set it next to my chair.

I was pretty sure he thought that I was crazy, but he was a waiter, so why should I give a fuck about his opinion? Maybe I was crazy. At the very least I knew that I'd lost my damn mind, but I'd known that before I'd decided to sit on the beach at sunset with oversized black sunglasses on to cry. I'd known that my mind was gone the moment the love of my life died in front of me. So while others probably whispered about the crazy lady who cried on the beach, I didn't care, because they had no idea what I was going through. Or what I'd been through. They could judge all they wanted, but walking a mile in my shoes would leave the average mu'fucka too broken to get out of bed in the morning. I'd earned the right to cry. I'd earned the right to mourn for the loss of my mom and dad, my first child, and my man, no matter how many might disagree. No matter how many tears I had to shed. The salty wetness on my face at this particular moment was a double-edged sword of grief and rage though. There was no doubt that I was wrapped in a blanket of darkness brought on by unspeakable pain, but the steady burning rage within kept the lights on. What had stirred the embers today was the newspaper article that I was currently reading on my tablet. Despite being out of the country, I stayed up on current events. The *Fort Worth Tribune* was reporting that after two weeks, there were still no leads on the shooting of prominent businessman Soloman Black or the shooting of his only daughter, Ivy Black. It gave a recap of both crimes and the troubles that had suddenly befallen the Black family as of late. My own family's troubles were nothing more than a side note, and Rockafella's death wasn't given a single letter in print. Not *one single letter*! It was obvious that someone was trying to erase the love I'd lost from the books of history, no doubt in an attempt to keep the image of Soloman and Ivy squeaky clean.

They weren't clean though. They were two of the dirtiest, grimiest mu'fuckas that had ever walked the earth, and they'd deserved to die. If given the opportunity, I'd kill them all over again today, and twice on Sunday! I knew that my anger and stress weren't any good for me or the baby that I was carrying, so I put the tablet aside while taking some much-needed deep breaths. The past couldn't be changed, but the future was still a blank canvas for me and my little bundle of joy, so that was what I would focus on. The thought of being a single mother made me more nauseous than my actual morning sickness, but what was the alternative?

No sooner had I asked myself this question than the face of the alternative popped into my mind, and with that face came feelings of stress for different reasons. The love I felt for Rockafella could never be called into question, but if a bitch had one weakness, it was for Justice. How else could I explain fucking him - on my wedding day, at that - and putting me in a situation where I was now like so many girls in the world who didn't know who their baby's daddy was? At the time, my justification for my actions had been that I was doing only what was necessary to save my husband's life, but in the light of day, I was forced to admit that that was some weak shit I'd sold myself to keep the guilt at bay. The ugly truth was that Justice made me a proposition that appealed to me on multiple levels. Saving Rock's life had been my priority, true enough, but lying on my back and spreading my legs for Justice had been something that I'd wanted for conflicting reasons. Whether it was me feenin' for the past, or wanting to reward his loyalty for his help in battling Ivy with me, it didn't really matter, because the result was the same. The father of my child was unknown.

I picked up my drink, intending to sip it while further wallowing in my misery, when my tablet started ringing with a FaceTime call. I automatically knew who it was, which meant I could keep hitting the ignore button or put my big girl panties on and face the music.

"I see that you're still as persistent as ever," I said after answering.

"You goddamn right, especially when I'm worried about you and don't know where the fuck you are!" Justice replied angrily.

I quickly turned my tablet around to give him a shot of my toes in the sand and the ocean in the distance before turning it back to face me.

"As you can see, I'm fine, but it's sweet of you to be worried. Especially considering that you're in the middle of all-out warfare."

"You know that I ain't new to this shit, and having a formidable opponent only makes it more interesting," he said, smirking evilly.

I knew there was some truth to his statement, just like I knew that he was trying to downplay the mess he was in. Justice was Piru, so he had an army behind him, especially on the West Coast. But he was battling two powerful enemies who wanted him dead in the worst way. I'd known Big Cuzz a long time because of his relationship with Ivy and his business relationship with my own father, so I knew that everything Hoover was riding with him against Justice right now. I didn't know the full extent of the Gulf Cartel's power, but the fact that they'd wiped out the Sinaloa Cartel *and* taken over their territory spoke volumes. With them on Justice's ass too, it only meant one thing. Death was a certainty, sooner rather than later.

"I think you should disappear for a while," I said.

"I don't do no running, EB, you know that."

"I'm not saying that you run away. I'm simply suggesting that you put some time and space between you and the fallout from what happened," I replied.

"I hear you, but I got niggas out here in the street dying for me right now, plus I got a lot of money moving too. I gotta stay in the trenches."

"You know that you can't spend money if you're dead, right?" I said, frustrated.

"Yeah, well, it ain't my time yet."

"Arrogant mu'fucka, how are you gonna say when it's your time to die? You ain't God!" I reminded him angrily.

"You're right, I'm not God, but I know God didn't take my son from me only to not allow me to see him serve up vengeance."

The pain in his voice told me just how raw his emotions were, and how close to the surface they were too. His pain was something that I could understand, but only in part. The child that I'd lost had barely started to grow in my stomach, but his son had been seven years old. That didn't mean that I loved my baby less than he had his son, but the love was different because of the time they'd spent together and the memories they'd shared. Despite the deaths of Ivy and Soloman, I could tell that for him, the score wasn't settled. I could only hope that his search for vengeance wasn't him knocking on death's door. A knock on that door only went unanswered for so long.

"I'm sorry that I wasn't there for your son's funeral," I said softly.

"You know that I understand you not being there. I can't lie though, it was the hardest thing that I ever had to do."

"I won't patronize you by telling you that it's somehow gonna get easier as time goes on because it's still an everyday fight with me and my grief," I admitted.

"Is that why you haven't been answering any of my calls?" he asked.

The look on his face was genuine concern, but I'd never doubted that he cared for me, so I wasn't surprised by it. I was, however, surprised by the sudden urge I felt to tell him the complete, uncensored truth.

"I've just been trying to get my mind right and figure out what I'm supposed to do next."

"And what have you come up with?" he asked.

"Not a goddamn thing. I'm lost right now," I confessed.

"Yeah, I know the feeling."

For a moment we simply stared at each other, speaking truths that hurt too much to verbalize while taking comfort in the fact that there was mutual understanding. This moment reminded me of the times when we would just lie in bed staring at each other, sometimes kissing, but mostly just communicating soul to soul. I actually felt myself smiling at the memory.

"What's funny?" he asked.

"Nothing. I was thinking about us when we were younger."

"That's dangerous. You better be careful going down that rabbit hole," he warned, chuckling.

We both knew that it was only dangerous because there was still chemistry between us, but I left that unsaid.

"Good memories are better than the alternative."

"I won't argue against that truth. Anyway, I just wanted to check on you, and now that I can see you're in one piece, I can get back to business," he said.

"Justice, business can wait. I'm sending my plane to get you."

"Not right now, EB, I - "

"Yes, *right now*. Haven't we both learned the hard way about taking time and people for granted?" I asked sincerely.

"I get that, but I'd be bad company right now, for real. I'm on some other shit."

I didn't need to ask him what he meant by that because the look in his eyes said it all. The pain was what he kept buried, but it was undoubtedly the power source behind the neon signs flashing murderous intent in his eyes. My concern was that those same intentions would lead to self-destruction, and that had me asking myself how I would feel if that happened. How would my baby feel if Justice turned out to be the father and I hadn't done everything I could to save him from himself? Regrets weren't something that I was in short supply of, but I really had no interest in adding to that pile.

"Justice, I understand what you're saying, but I could really use you out here right now."

"EB, I love you, but I'm in no condition to hand hold," he said honestly.

"That's okay because I can hold my own hand, but it would be nice to have someone to hold my hair back when I throw up. Morning sickness is a bitch."

"M-morning sickness? That would mean… You mean you're - "

"Yes, I'm pregnant, and as my luck would have it, I don't know whose baby I'm carrying. Now since you played a big role in putting me in this position, I think that the *least* you could do is be here for me when you know that I'm an emotional basket case," I said seriously.

"Y-you're pregnant? You know this for sure, or are you speculating because you missed a period?"

"It's only been two weeks since all hell broke loose so if I was just late, I wouldn't have told you that the baby might be yours. The truth is that I knew I was pregnant *before* I did what you asked. When you called and demanded that I come see you, I'd just left my doctor's office. We'd thought that I was going in for a routine check-up post-surgery, but when the doctor did an ultrasound, he found out that I was pregnant," I replied.

Those same hazel eyes that had held the threat of bloodshed moments before were now doing rapid calculation, and it looked like the math made him suddenly human again.

"Why didn't you tell me when you came to Cali?" he asked.

"You know that would've been the *worst* time to tell you some shit like that, not to mention how ugly shit would've gotten between you and Rock."

"So if he was still alive, would you have ever told me, or would you have simply let another nigga raise a child that's possibly mine?" he asked with edge in his voice.

15

"Check your tone, Justice. I know that this is a messy situation, but I'm far from a messy bitch, and I don't appreciate you coming at me like I'm that type of female."

He may have wanted to get slick out the mouth, but he swallowed whatever words he had on his tongue and just looked at me.

"Where are you?" he asked finally.

"The question is, where are *you*?" I retorted, trying to gain some insight from the bedroom in the background. One thing I knew for sure was that it definitely looked like a project spot.

"I'm in Oakland."

"I'll send the plane," I stated.

"Text me the details."

"I got you," I replied, preparing to disconnect.

"Hey, EB…Thank you," he said genuinely.

As badly as my heart hurt, it felt good to be able to inspire hope inside him. Maybe it would, in turn, inspire hope in me, because I knew that I had a long road in front of me, and for my child's sake, I couldn't wallow in depression. No matter how badly I wanted to.

"I'll see you soon," I said, touching my fingers to my lips before putting them to the screen.

When his face disappeared, I took a deep breath and a long drink of my banana daiquiri. I quickly made the necessary arrangements for my plane to go to Oakland, and after watching the remainder of the sun setting, I stood up to make my way back to my villa. I had no idea how long it would take Justice to get out here, but a bitch definitely wasn't about to wait up for him.

When I got back to the villa, I ordered a nice lobster dinner, ate it, and then ran myself a bubble bath. All of this would've probably had most women feeling like something special to be in this exotic paradise and have whatever at your fingertips. For me, I was simply going through the motions because it was all of no importance anymore.

Once my bath was finished, I went straight to bed and waited on sleep to come. Most nights it was impossible to find the land of blissful slumber until the moon was high in the sky, but miraculously, I found myself beyond the world's reach shortly after my head hit the pillow. My dreams were of my handsome husband, and I was actually happy, but too soon, it was ripped away by the feeling of a hand clamping down forcefully on my mouth.

"Don't move and don't breathe, bitch. You've got a date with Ivy."

Aryanna

Chapter 2
Ivy
Texas

"How do you feel?"

"Like I'm dying," I replied weakly.

"Well, Ms. Black, you may be dead to the world, but I can assure you that you're very much alive."

I looked to Big for some type of explanation to the riddles this doctor was speaking in, but all I saw on his face was complete and utter relief.

"Do you remember what happened?" the doctor asked, flipping through the medical chart in his hand.

"I got-got shot."

"Actually, you were shot twice: once in the chest and once in the head," the doctor corrected.

"I was shot in the-the head? Does that mean - "

"It's okay, Ms. Black, the bullet to your head only grazed your scalp. The one to your chest was worse because it hit a piece of your heart, and that required emergency surgery. Obviously the fact that you woke up signifies that, so far, the surgery is proving to be a success, but we will still be monitoring you closely. Do you remember who shot you?" he asked.

I didn't look directly at Big, but I didn't have to in order to see his subtle head shake. The truth was that I hadn't forgotten a mu'fuckin' thing, least of all what questions I could answer.

"No, I don't know who shot me," I replied.

"Okay, I'll be sure to let the police know so that they won't come in and bother you. I'll be back in about an hour or so to check on you," the doctor said, putting my chart down and leaving my room.

"I can tell by the look on your face that I must've been close to death's door," I said, looking at Big.

"I don't want to talk about that."

"How long have I been in the hospital?" I asked.

"It's been two weeks."

"No wonder my breath tastes awful," I said, grimacing.

I'd expected at least a slight smile from my man, but I got nothing except the haunted look of a man who'd almost lost everything.

"I'm okay, Big."

"But you weren't, Ivy. You damn near died," he replied.

I could hear the anger in his voice, but I didn't understand why it would be directed at me.

"Are you really mad at me right now?" I asked, looking at him closer.

For a moment his eyes spoke the words that he didn't want to, but I knew his restraint was only because I'd just woken up from the longest nap of my life.

"Say something, Big."

"What do you want me to say, Ivy? That I'm mad? No, I'm not mad, I'm fucking *pissed*, and yeah, some of that anger is directed at you," he admitted.

"Why though, babe?"

"Because you didn't listen to me, Ivy. You chose to do shit your own way instead of taking the advice I gave you, and it almost cost you your life. You can't have feelings if you're gonna survive in this game, so when a bitch threatens you, that means you can't give her the benefit of the doubt. You can't reason with her either. You can only eliminate her, because even with eyes in the back of your head, you can't see everything that's coming. How much do you have to lose to understand this?" he asked seriously.

20

"Trust me, I get it now."

I could tell by the expression on his face that he wasn't convinced. But he wasn't feeling the same pain that I was right now. I hadn't grown up with conscious thoughts of what getting shot would feel like, and even if I had, no amount of creative imagining would've prepared me for reality's pain. I *never* wanted to experience this shit again, so while Big might have doubts about my ability to say fuck any bitch or nigga, I was absolute about my decision.

"Where's Darlise?" I asked.

"I ain't seen her since she came running out of the hotel."

"How do the police not know who shot me? I know there were cameras in the hotel," I said, confused.

"Because they were paid not to know, just like they were paid to say that you'd been killed," he replied.

"They actually went along with that?"

"It made sense for them to go along with you being dead given everything that's happened to your family recently. As far as not identifying Darlise, I explained to Chief Stringer that it had to be handled in the street," he replied.

The way he'd said that gave me chills, so I could only imagine how the chief of police had felt being in Big's presence. Normally he tried to keep the fact that he was a cold killer hidden beneath the surface of his gentle 6'5", two hundred fifty pound frame, but there was no hiding his truth right now. I'd known and loved him long enough to know that he was gonna kill everything moving until he felt righteous again.

"What did my dad say about this? He's probably angrier than you are," I said with dread.

He'd warned me about the need to grow eyes in the back of my head so that I could watch everybody, so I knew that I was in for one hell of a lecture when I got home.

"Big, did you hear me?" I asked when he didn't respond.

For a moment, I thought he was ignoring me because he was still mad, but the look on his face was slightly different. There was anger there, but it also looked like guilt mixed in with it, and that made me uneasy.

"Baby," I said fearfully.

When he still didn't speak, I knew what he couldn't say, and the immense pain that instantly took ahold of me made my gunshot wounds feel like paper cuts.

"H-how?" I asked, fighting against the urge to sob.

"Ebony."

"Oh-oh God, no," I moaned weakly.

The knowledge that flooded my brain no longer allowed me to control the urge to cry, and trying to suppress the volume of my wails with a hand over my mouth still didn't stop the tears. Losing my father was one thing, but the fact that he'd died at Ebony's hand meant *I* was the one who actually killed him. I now understood the guilt that Big felt, but in my soul, I knew that burden was mine. All mine.

It was a while before I was able to see through the rivers running from my eyes, and the screams in my throat subsided enough to prevent me having to be sedated for hysteria. I still know that despite calming down I was far from in control, but the feeling of Big's hand in mine gave me the strength that I desperately needed in this moment. Neither of us spoke, yet we knew there was plenty to say. I knew he was waiting on me though, giving me time to get to shore while understanding that I was swimming against the current of my tsunami-sized emotions. In my heart I knew that there would be many more days and nights of inconsolable tears after this loss, but in this moment, I knew that my father would expect me to lock my emotions away. He would expect me to keep on pushing.

"Tell me what happened," I said, reaching for the cup of water sitting on the tray in front of me.

"It happened while we were meeting up with Darlise. According to your head of security, James, Rock, and Ebony came into the house like normal, and while Rock went upstairs, Ebony went to your father's room. A couple minutes later, James heard a gunshot and came running. He saw Rock standing outside your dad's room and he put one in his head without hesitation. Ebony came out shooting, managing to kill your dad's nurse before getting away."

Hearing that that slippery bitch had somehow managed to escape gave me equal feelings of disappoint and pleasure. Disappointment for obvious reasons, but at least now I know that I'd have the pleasure of watching her take her last breath. I wouldn't rest until that happened.

"Where is she?" I asked.

"I'm actually waiting on confirmation that we have her because I just found out that she's in Aruba."

"Well, it looks like I woke up just in time then. Should I assume that Justice is hiding his sister?" I asked disgustedly.

"Of course you know that that's the first person Darlise would run to, especially because we had the press on her ass a couple hours after you got shot."

"He's actually protecting this bitch *knowing* that she's the one who betrayed him and caused his son to die? And here I thought that I was the only one who was stupid enough to forgive the unforgivable," I said, shaking my head.

"I'd say that it's a safe bet that Justice doesn't *know* that Darlise betrayed him. You already know that she damn sure ain't gonna volunteer that information," he replied.

I processed this information in silence and filed it away in my mind for later use.

"What's the status on Justice?"

"So far he's survived, but he knows that his days are numbered. My team is on his ass, plus Juanito has personally been leading the cartel up into Cali," he replied.

"I thought Manuel didn't want us involved in any street shit," I said sarcastically.

"Yeah, well, that was before you got shot. Once that happened, he knew that there was no way I'd sit on the sideline, which meant that it only made good business sense for him to get involved. Plus he knew that I blamed him for everything, and that I'd kill him if he *didn't* get involved."

"And how would he know that?" I asked carefully.

Big didn't answer, but the smirk on his face said it all.

"Baby, I know that you're a bad mu'fucka, but please don't threaten the head of the cartel," I said.

"I'm not making no promises, except that if him or his people fuck up again, I'm not wasting any more words or time. I'ma kill him."

I knew he was serious, which meant that there was no need to try talking him out of it. The best thing that I could do was keep him focused on our real enemies.

"I need you to keep Ebony on ice until I'm released from the hospital. I gotta have her myself," I stated.

"That goes without saying, but she will be severely tortured and violated until that time comes."

"Aww, baby, thank you," I said genuinely.

Seeing something that actually passed for a smile cross his face made it slightly easier to breathe. I was too deep under the water of my emotions to be able to deal with him being angry at me.

"I've been handling business in your absence, and you'll be happy to know that we've had too much pressure on Justice for him to focus on his play for the ports. That don't mean that he's forgot a damn thing, but I'ma make him understand that dead men can't spend money," he stated adamantly.

"To be honest, I'm surprised that he's managed to elude the pressure that you and Juanito have put on him."

"He's got some loyal niggas that've laid down their life for him, and apparently he had the money to buy more," Big replied, clearly frustrated by that fact.

"I didn't know that his money was that long. Or does he have a backer?" I asked thoughtfully.

"I was thinking the same thing because we know that Ebony's hoe ass would run straight to him now that Rock is dead. So far there haven't been any sightings of them together, and that nigga wouldn't dream of vacationing right now. Staying and moving through projects that are familiar to him is what's saved his miserable fucking life up to this point."

"She don't gotta see him to get money to him, but I'll be sure to get that information out of her before I kill her," I vowed.

"You do know that I'm gonna have to insist that you focus on getting better before anything, right?" he asked.

What I knew was that it was pointless to argue with this stubborn-ass nigga, but thankfully the doctor coming back in spared me from having to try. The sight of an older white lady accompanying him caused a slight feeling of nervousness to surge through me, but I didn't panic.

"Ms. Black, I'm Dr. Lorraine Paddington, and I'm consulting with Dr. Stevens on your case," she said.

"Okay, well I guess that I can use all the help that I can get," I replied honestly.

The sudden ringing of Big's phone diverted all of our attention, but he quickly excused himself to answer it.

"So what's next, Doc?" I asked, looking from one to the other.

"Well, now that you're awake, my concern is getting you the right pain medications that will help with your discomfort without having lasting effects," Dr. Paddington said.

"Okay, that's good, because I definitely don't want to develop an addiction to pain medications," I replied seriously.

"I'm sure you don't, and part of my specialty as an OB-GYN is figuring out the proper meds that will work well with your vitamin regimen," Dr. Paddington said, nodding encouragingly.

"I'm sorry, did you say that you're an OBGYN?" I asked, confused.

They exchanged a quick look before she nodded again.

"I don't understand," I said slowly.

"Well, part of your admission treatment is extensive blood work, and when we did yours, we discovered that you were pregnant," Dr. Stevens said.

"What?" I asked softly, feeling the grief that I'd thought I'd suppressed resurface with more intensity.

Only my father had known how desperately I'd wanted to have a baby with Big, and how I'd been stressing the fact that it hadn't happened despite me no longer being on birth control. To have to suffer through the loss of my daddy and my baby was too much for God to ask of me. I'd prefer to swallow a fast-moving bullet.

"I can tell that you're surprised to learn about your pregnancy, but that's not unusual when it's still early on," Dr. Paddington said.

"Early?" I repeated.

"Six weeks, based on our tests," she said.

Knowing that my baby was still in the first trimester of life didn't soften the blow of the loss.

"Your case is actually a miracle," Dr. Stevens said.

"A-a miracle? *What*?" I asked, fighting the urge to hop out of my bed and hop on his Goddamn helmet.

"A miracle, Ms. Black. I can't tell you how many women lose their babies when they have to undergo massive surgery, especially for something as serious a gunshot. So for you and your baby to make it through that is nothing short of a miracle," Dr. Paddington said in agreement.

For a moment I had to stare at them because I wasn't sure that I was hearing what they were saying instead of it being what I wanted to hear. The kind smile on Dr. Paddington's face gave me hope though.

"Are you-are you saying that I'm still pregnant? That my baby is still alive?" I asked slowly.

"Alive and healthy for you being two months along," Dr. Stevens replied.

"Does-does my husband know?" I asked.

"No. At my insistence, Dr. Stevens agreed to wait until we knew what was going on with you, but we would've told him if your circumstances would've changed for the worse, and he would've had to decide on your life or death," Dr. Paddington said.

That meant that Big was about to get one *hell* of a surprise when he came back.

"Okay, so now what happens?" I asked.

"Well, now I'm gonna examine you thoroughly, but I'm gonna have you brought over to the maternity side of the hospital where all my tools are," Dr. Paddington replied.

"And then when she's finished, I'll be back to check your wounds," Dr. Stevens stated.

"Okay," I said.

"Alright, someone will be along shortly to bring you to me," Dr. Paddington said.

They both left the room, and Big walked in a few moments later. Looking at him now, I didn't know how I was gonna tell him, but it was obvious good news was needed.

"What's wrong?" I asked.

"We got a problem."

Chapter 3
Ebony

Fear had my body frozen rigid, but my mind was running faster than Usain Bolt. I wanted this all to be a bad dream, but the look in his eyes was too real to be fake, and the weight of his body on mine only made it realer. That meant his statement about me having a date with a dead woman only meant one thing for me and my baby. Just as I was preparing to offer any and everything to have our lives spared, a shadow moved in my peripheral vision, and the nigga on top of me was hit like he played in the NFL. I had no idea who'd just tackled him, but I was up and out of the bed before both bodies hit the floor on the other side of the bed. My instincts were screaming at me to get the fuck out of Dodge in a hurry, but instead I hit the light switch so my savior could see what he was doing. My recognition of Justice was immediate, but I had no idea who the nigga was under him catching a vicious ass whooping. I'd never heard a mu'fuckin' hit that was hard enough to break someone's facial bones until now. With one punch I saw the right eye that had just been blazing with determination and anger inches away from mine sink into his face as the orbital bone holding it up shattered beneath the skin.

"Don't holler now!" Justice said, still swinging.

His next two punches made blood fly, and now there was a dazed look in the man's eyes.

"D-don't kill him. I wanna know who sent him," I said, moving towards them.

"Sent him? What do you mean? I thought he was trying to rape you," Justice replied, looking at me in confusion.

"He said that I had a date with Ivy, and that means somebody sent him," I said.

Hearing this made Justice fire another bone shattering right hook that left our mystery guest on the verge of consciousness.

"Who sent you?" he asked angrily.

"F-fuck you," the man replied weakly.

It was on the tip of my tongue to tell Justice not to feed into what he said, but he'd already hit him again, knocking him out cold.

"Are you okay?" Justice asked, looking at me with eyes now full of concern.

"Yeah, I'm okay. Where the hell did you come from though?"

"Your guardian angel was definitely watching over you because I pulled up just in time to see this nigga creeping through your living room. Sure, it could've been someone that you were fucking, but I doubted that you'd have another nigga around knowing that I was on my way out here. So that meant dude was up to no good. I came in through the same balcony door that he used," Justice replied.

"God, it's good to see you," I said, finally allowing the relief I felt to consume me.

He gave me that long smile that I remembered as he climbed off of the still-snoring man under him and came towards me. The moment his arms wrapped around me I felt myself start to tremble, but I knew that I was safe, despite the fact that Ivy was reaching beyond the grave to snatch me down.

"Who do you think sent him?" I asked.

"My money is on Big Cuzz. That nigga has been on a war path since Ivy died, and *anybody* can get it."

"You say that like you've been living a lot closer to the edge than I thought," I said, looking up at him.

"It ain't nothing that I can't handle. Believe it or not, the nigga who took over for Gangsta Bit is just as ruthless as his predecessor, and he loves warfare as much as I do."

"You mean as much as you *used* to, right? If this baby I'm carrying is yours, you already know that your focus and priorities have gotta be different if you want to be a part of our lives," I said seriously.

"Please don't talk to me like you didn't just knock Soloman's head off a couple weeks ago."

His words forced me to step out of his embrace, but I bit back the words that I wanted to sling at him. The reality was that he was telling the truth. I had blood on my hands. But during these last two weeks, I'd committed to living a different life for my baby's sake. I needed him to be on the same page.

"You're right, I shot Soloman, and not just because you asked me to. For me, Soloman's and Ivy's deaths completed the circle of events, and so now I can move on with my life," I said.

"While the rest of us deal with the fallout, huh?"

"Justice, don't try to make this seem like it's my fault that you're still at war with Big and the cartel because it was you're decision to go after Ivy's empire. You're involvement in this shit stopped being about me the moment you left Texas and went back to Cali," I replied.

Now it was his turn to remain silent in the face of the truth. I wouldn't try to downplay anything that Justice had done for me, but we both knew that his greed had led him to where he was at now.

"I can understand you wanting to give our child the best possible life, but you have to understand that you don't get a clean slate just because you're pregnant or because you want one. Have you ever stopped to ask yourself why you're never been named as a suspect in Soloman's murder? For the same reason that my sister ain't been fingered for Ivy's murder. Because those who are avenging them want to kill you *themselves*. There's your proof right there," he said, pointing to the unconscious man on the floor.

It was hard not to listen to what he was saying when I could still taste the fear on my tongue from my most recent brush with death.

"We both agree that this ain't the life we want for this baby, so what do we do? I've got the money and means to run, but are you willing to do that?" I asked.

"Do you really think that there's anywhere we can hide, sweetheart? We're fighting with people who have the same unlimited resources, and a matching determination to see us stop breathing."

"So what do you suggest then?" I asked, becoming more frustrated.

"It's gonna sound crazy, but we've gotta go back to Cali."

My immediate response was to look at him and blink real slow while waiting on the punch line to his joke. When he didn't deliver one in thirty seconds, I began fearing that he was actually being serious.

"You really have lost your damn mind if that's your solution," I said seriously.

"That's because you're still thinking like a square. How do we protect ourselves halfway around the world with no army surrounding us? And if you were to go somewhere, how do you expect me to focus knowing that you and our baby are out there unprotected?"

"So you want us on the frontline instead? That still seems crazy," I said.

"EB, we're in a fucked-up situation, and that means conventional thinking can't be applied if we're gonna survive. I just need you to trust me."

My indecision wasn't because I was apprehensive about putting my trust in Justice. I was just tired of this street shit. This wasn't supposed to be how my life turned out, but I hadn't envisioned me being an orphaned, single mother who was a college dropout and a cold blooded killer either. It was becoming clear to me that my life now embodied the meaning behind the saying that the only way out was through.

"I trust you, Justice."

"Good, because we need to get the fuck out of here ASAP. There's no telling how many goons Big sent at you now that he knows your location," he replied, going back to our still-sleeping guest.

"I'll call and refuel the plane for immediate takeoff," I said, going to the living room to get my phone.

I made the phone call, offering a nice bonus if they could have the plane ready within the hour. Once I was done I went back into the bedroom, where I walked into a sight I really didn't wanna see.

"Where did you get a gun?" I asked.

"It's his, and I don't have to tell you what his intentions were for it."

"So what are you gonna do with it? Because you know we can't clear airport security with it," I said.

In response, he straddled the man, raised the pistol, and smacked him in the mouth with it, knocking out three teeth like window panes.

"Well, that's one way to wake him up," I said, shaking my head as I began to get dressed and gather my shit together.

"Are you ready to tell me who sent you?" I heard Justice ask.

I didn't hear the man's reply, but his sudden screams of pain gave me a good idea of what he'd said. While Justice focused on that, I did my best to pack my shit so it didn't look like I'd vanished in the middle of the night. With any luck, they'd assume that I stayed through my month long rental, and since my maid service was only done by request, there was nobody to say otherwise. I made it back into the bedroom just in time to see Justice jam the barrel of the Glock .40 in between the man's lips.

"I - " I said in warning.

"You got all your shit together?"

"Yeah, and by the time we get to the airport, the plane will be ready, so let's go," I replied.

"A'ight, I'll be right there."

"Come on, Justice, knock him out and let's go."

"Knock him out? He came in here with the intention of hurting you and our child, Ebony. Do you know what would've happened if I hadn't been here? I mean, who knows what type of foul shit this nigga was told to do to you," he said.

I definitely didn't want to think about that, but I could tell that Justice was living in the thought of how real shit could've gotten, and it had that madness swimming in his eyes again.

"I-I'm okay, so - "

The roar of the gun froze my speech, and the explosion of the man's head made whatever I had to say pointless. Justice calmly wiped his prints off the gun before putting it on the man's chest and standing up. It was hard to ignore the blood splatter on his shirt as he walked over to me and took the bag from my hand, but I did.

"Let's go," he said calmly.

"You gotta get rid of that shirt before we get to the airport," I stated, following him out front to his rental car.

He quickly changed shirts, and then we got on the move. Forty-five minutes later we were inside the safety of my G3, racing down the runway as the sun began to peek over the trees looming in front of us in the darkness. I didn't take a deep breath until the plane had leveled off, but I knew that my anxiety and apprehension would come back once we touched down on American soil. It was crazy that I was more afraid now then I had been when Ivy was alive, and we'd been going head to head. She'd definitely turned out to be more ruthless than I'd given her credit for, but Big was a different animal. Death and war were what he lived for, and I had no doubt that Ivy's death was more motivation.

"Thank you, Justice. I don't know what would've happened if you hadn't been there."

"I'm always gonna do everything I can to make sure I'm there for you. Both of you," he replied sincerely, pulling me into his arms.

I didn't think that any man could ever make me feel safe in their arms besides Rock, but there was no other way to describe what I felt when I was wrapped up in Justice. For a while he simply held me, and I was content. When his hand slipped under my T-shirt and rested on my stomach, I tensed up though, unsure of what to think or feel. When I looked up at him, I saw the tears and pain in his eyes, and it made my heart ache for him. It wasn't a conscious intention on my part to kiss him or to allow him to kiss me, but suddenly our lips were touching and I had no idea who'd made the first move. I know that it was need that made me open my mouth to his, seeking out the comfort of his tongue like a favorite pair of slippers. Our kisses were soft, patient while being passionate, and thorough enough to have my pussy wide awake with growing excitement. When his hand moved from my stomach and inched its way into my shorts and panties, I didn't tense up. I actually opened my legs to allow him room to play.

"You're soaking wet," he whispered against my lips.

"Side effect of pregnancy."

The steady motion of his middle finger inside me had my body heating up with unchecked desire, but when he stretched the tightness of my pussy by adding another finger, I was gripped by fierce need.

"Enough playing," I said, wiggling out of my shorts and moving around to straddle him.

When he grabbed me by my hips and lifted me, I quickly unzipped his Dickies, and pulled his dick out. With hurried movements, I pulled my panties to the side so that he could answer me onto what I knew would take my mind far away from life's dramas.

"Go slow," he said, holding me close.

Once I had him completely inside me, that was the last thing I wanted to do, but I understood that sex was never simply sex with him and I. My rhythm of rise and fall was as patient as our kisses had been, but my pussy was still throbbing with reinforced need within minutes. The feeling of his lips walking up my neck were as hypnotizing as the feeling of his heart beating against my chest, and by the time his tongue touched my ear lobe I was under his spell. The way his hands alternated between caressing and

squeezing my ass cheeks had me moving with more pur-
pose.

"You feel so good," he whispered passionately.

"Y-you too, babe."

Even with me moving at a slow and steady rhythm, my
first orgasm still hit me with the force of severe turbulence,
making me cling to him tighter.

"Oh-oh fuck," he moaned.

I could hear the worry in his voice and I knew it was
because my pussy was now too wet for him to comprehend.
This made me ride him faster, closing my eyes and allowing the dick to take me where I wanted to go.

"F-fuck or get f-fucked," I moaned, moving steadily
faster.

Suddenly I found myself on my back on the leather
loveseat we'd been on, and I knew that my challenge was
accepted. The power behind his long strokes had my toes
curling and I could see my climax rushing towards me up
out of the darkness.

"Oh, h-harder!" I demanded, clawing at his back
through his T-shirt.

Without warning, he bent me in half, and I found myself beneath him getting dicked down in jackhammer fash-
ion.

"Ugh! Fuck!" I exclaimed in ecstasy, even as tears
leaked from my eyes.

For untold minutes he pounded my pussy like he owned
it, and I rewarded him by cumming all over him again in
an uncontrollable wave of heat. In the middle of my own
climax, I felt his dick vibrating with the intensity of the en-
gine outside our window, and then I felt the explosion of
him deep inside me. The fact that the tears that had been in
his eyes were now on his cheeks told me that he felt what I

did, and no words could explain what had just happened. I could see the love he felt for not only the child inside me, but for me as well, and it felt amazing to know that someone in this world could still love me. I knew that no matter what happened after this, Justice would love me through it.

I could tell it was with great reluctance that he pulled out of me, but he wasted no time pulling me into his arms, and that's where I was when sleep came to claim me. This time when I dreamed it wasn't of Rock, but it was of a baby that looked just like him. I awoke with a looming feeling of uncertainty that I couldn't quite explain, but I knew immediately that that wasn't what had disturbed my sleep. The sudden tension radiating from Justice was palpable and comparable to a concerned rattlesnake.

"Is-is everything alright?" I asked.

"Yeah."

I could hear the lie without looking at his face, but I still leaned back to look at him.

"What is it, J?"

"I know how Ivy found out about my son."

Chapter 4
Ivy

"What's the problem?" I asked.

"Somehow Ebony managed to kill one of the men I sent to get her in Aruba."

"Exactly how does that happen? Because the last time I checked, she wasn't built to handle a confrontation with one of yours," I said.

"My other homie believes that she had some help. He was waiting down on the beach by the boat when he heard a gunshot. By the time he got to the house, there was nobody there. Just my dead homie."

"I'm sorry to hear about the homie, but how does any of that translate into Ebony having help?" I asked, confused.

"Ebony didn't have a car, but somehow her *and* all of her shit had vanished by the time my man got from the beach to the house. That means unless that bitch knows magic and rides a broomstick, she had some help, and we both know who that help would be," he replied, giving me a knowing look.

Apparently the belief that Justice wouldn't take a vacation in Aruba right now was proving to be false.

"When was the last time someone actually saw Justice?" I asked.

"Two days ago, I believe, but I'll double check that."

Our conversation was interrupted by a nurse's arrival with a wheelchair. "You ready to go, Ms. Black?" the short redhead asked.

"How long will this take? Because my husband has somewhere to be, and I don't want him to leave while I'm gone," I said.

"Let me check real quick," she replied, retreating the way she'd come.

"Husband?" Big asked with a questioning look and a teasing smile.

"Yeah, nigga, we're getting married because I'm not having my baby out of wedlock like some random hood nigger bitch."

"Oh, so it's not about the fact that you're in love with me?" he asked with mock hurt.

"Don't be dramatic," I replied, smiling.

"I'm just saying, if you wanna get married now, being in love would be nice, because if you're waiting until you get pregnant, then we've got a while."

"Not as long as you think," I replied cryptically.

"Oh, so now you're saying that you wanna have my baby too? Shit, if all I had to do was shoot you to get you to fully commit to a nigga, I would've put a bullet in your ass a long time ago!"

"So what are you saying? You *want* to get married and you *want* me to have your baby?" I asked, fighting hard to keep a straight face.

"Baby, I've wanted that since the first time I laid eyes on you. Have I ever given you the impression that this thing wasn't forever for me?"

"No, but we've never had a serious conversation about what forever would look like for us, and now shit is just so different."

"You're right, it is different, because before, I wasn't as conscious of how fragile and fleeting life really is. My eyes are open to that now, and so since we're having a real conversation, I'ma be all the way real with you by telling you that I want you forever. I want some little mini versions of you too," he declared sincerely.

"Ms. Black, Dr. Paddington said your exam shouldn't take long because it'll only be a blood draw and ultrasound," the nurse said, coming back into my room.

"Ultrasound? Don't you mean chest X-ray?" Big asked, confused.

"Um, that's not what the doctor just said on the phone, and I am about to wheel her to the maturity ward, so…" the nurse replied, looking back and forth between me and Big.

When Big looked at me, his eyes were full of questions, and now it was my turn to smile.

"Like I said, we don't got as long as you think, so you might wanna start making arrangements, *husband*," I stated.

"You're *not* pregnant right now," he whispered in awe.

"Yes, she is," the nurse blurted out.

"You heard the nurse, and you know that she doesn't know me to lie for me," I said, smiling wider.

The fact that the revelation of me being pregnant made this thorough-ass gangsta misty-eyed instantly made me want to laugh, but it was too endearing to mock. He slowly leaned over, and I was immediately mortified because I knew he was about to kiss me while my breath was hot, but the look in his eyes said that he wouldn't be denied. I tried to keep it light, but his mouth assaulted mine in a way that caused pleasure to ignite within my body like I'd swallowed lit rocket fuel. I'm pretty sure that the nurse's heavy breathing was the only thing that reminded Big that we weren't alone, and therefore couldn't try for twins.

"You must truly love me because you just tongued me down when I have the worst breath ever," I said, chuckling.

"Tasted like the sweetest forever to me," he replied, smiling.

"Awww," the nurse moaned.

I started to tell this bitch to mind her business because she was intruding on a moment, but this situation was truly too beautiful for me to get ugly.

"Wait for me," I said, giving Big a wink.

"You never have to tell me that twice," he replied.

When I turned my attention on the nurse, she blushed with guilt at having been caught in our business instead of taking care of hers, but she quickly began to unhook my IV. She and Big both helped me into the wheelchair as I fought against the pain that seemed to echo through my chest. At this point, I didn't know who I wanted to kill worse - Darlise or Ebony - but the pain that I was feeling right now gave me an idea.

"You know, maybe it's time Justice knows how word of his little man came my way. I'm sure that would shift his focus for a minute," I said, giving Big a knowing look.

"I'll handle it," he replied shortly.

After he kissed me one more time briefly, the nurse rolled me out of the room and down to the maternity wing. The sound of babies crying in the distance was the sweetest sound in the world to me, and it gave me a hope that I'd never known. Losing my father was still crushing me, but somehow I felt like this was God's way of opening a window after he'd closed a door. The entire time that Dr. Paddington examined me, I just kept thinking about the conversation that I'd had with my dad about my fears because I wasn't pregnant yet after months of trying. His sage advice and wisdom was to be patient because becoming a mother would happen on God's time had filled my heart with love then, as it did now. Of course the moment was bittersweet though because my child would never get to meet his or her grandparents, but would definitely know about them.

I felt like an idiot for lying on the exam table and crying during my entire checkup. It was obvious that the doctor was used to this response because she simply passed me some tissues and kept right on doing her thing. When it was all said and done, she gave me a prescription for a pain medication that wouldn't harm my baby, and plenty of pre-natal vitamins to take to keep us both healthy. The same nurse that had transported me down here took me back to my room, but as soon as we crossed the threshold, she pulled up short.

"W-what's wrong?' I asked Big, looking from him to the four man entourage holding up the wall next to him.

"Nothing is wrong. We're good," he replied.

The nurse still didn't push me any further into the room, and I didn't have to look back at her to know that she was spooked by the presence of some stone-faced killers.

"Okay, so if nothing's wrong, then can you please ex-plain this party we're having?" I said.

"We're taking you home," Big stated.

"She can't leave the hospital without the doctor's ap-proval," the nurse informed him.

"Do I look like the type that needs anyone's approval for any reason?" Big asked.

He'd phrased this question using a normal tone of voice, but I knew that look in his eye.

"Baby, she's just doing her job," I said, wheeling my-self towards where he was standing.

I could hear the nurse back out of the room quickly, and I prayed that she knew better than to call security on these niggas.

"Y'all know that you're scaring the white people, right?" I asked, looking good at Big's homies.

I wasn't surprised that these niggas actually had the nerve to smile, which was why I shook my head and turned my attention back on Big.

They ain't come to scare the white folks. They're just here to make sure that you get home safely," Big said.

"If I recall correctly, you said that everyone thinks that I'm already dead, so why so much protection?" I asked.

"Because I ain't taking no chances with your life or our baby," he stated.

"Ah," I replied, seeing clearly how the next seven months was gonna go.

"Don't worry, I've already hired two nurses to look after you at home, and they've agreed to live-in despite the noise inconvenience," Big said.

"Noise inconvenience?" I asked, raising a quizzical eyebrow.

"Yeah, there's a little construction going on at the Big house right now. I had a fifteen foot high brick wall that's reinforced with steel put around the property," he replied nonchalantly.

"Did you say at my parents' house, or down on the Mexican border?" I asked chuckling.

"Laugh all you want, it's still happening," he replied seriously.

"Babe, there's no way that you arranged all of this in the short amount of time that I was out of this room."

"Not the wall. That's been under construction for about a week and a half. I did just arrange to have it completed within seventy-two hours though," he said.

"So what's your plan, baby, to lock me away in a tower?" I asked, still giggling despite the pain.

"Don't worry, my queen, you'll get the royal treatment."

"Ms. Black, what's going on here?" Dr. Stevens asked from behind me.

"What's going on is that I'm taking her home, where she will be cared for around the clock," Big stated.

"She can't - "

"What?" Big asked, his voice soft but unmistakably threatening.

"S-she shouldn't leave just yet, considering that she just regained consciousness a little while ago," Dr. Stevens replied nervously.

"Doc, I respect your medical opinion. I think that you should respect how *final* my decision is," Big said.

His emphasis of the word "final" didn't escape my notice, which meant that it damn sure didn't go over the doctor's head. If he'd known Big at all, then he'd know that the look he was getting right now was indicative of my man's willingness to put a bullet in anyone who tried to fuck with his agenda. It was obvious to me that I needed to step in and save the doctor from himself.

"Doctor Stevens, I'm sure that you can understand my husband's desire to have me home where he can hover over me and nurse me back to health. I would appreciate you examine me before I leave though," I said, spinning my wheelchair around to face him.

The indecision on his face was clear to see, but I was counting on his intelligence to prevail in this situation.

"I-I do need to examine you, but, uh - "

"Two outside in the hall and two by the car," Big said, anticipating the doctor's next words.

The men moved without a word, leaving Big, me, and the doctor. I could tell by the look on Dr. Stevens's face that he wanted Big to leave too, but everyone in the room knew that wasn't gonna happen.

"Can you get back into the bed please?" the doctor requested.

With Big's help, I did as he asked, and ten minutes later, the doctor was gone to take care of the necessary discharge paperwork.

"You're so *mean*," I said once we were alone.

"I prefer the word determined."

"I don't give a damn what you prefer. I know what I just witnessed," I replied, laughing.

"It could've been worse."

"True. So now what? I mean, it's obvious that you've taken control of my life now," I said, accepting my new reality.

"Well, you'll be happy to know that I took care of making sure that Justice knows that there's a fox in the hen house, and I should know where they're at shortly," he replied.

"How's that?"

"The same way that I tracked her to Aruba. The tail number on her daddy's plane," he said.

"What, have you been watching spy movies or something?" I asked, amazed that he thought of that.

"Nah, I just ain't about to be outsmarted by someone who's playing at being a gangsta."

"I can understand that. What do you say we get out of here?" I suggested, wanting to be home now as badly as Big wanted me there.

"Sounds like a plan."

I'd thought that him helping me get dressed would be a problem simply because of the pain that I was in, but the real issue was in the fact that he decided to stick his fingers inside me while helping me with my pants. My mouth told him to quit playing, but my pussy sang for him like Rihanna. Before I knew it, I had to clamp a hand over my mouth because the door to the room was open, and I didn't want someone to overhear me cumming.

"You-you're so wrong for that," I whispered.

"If you think that now, just wait until I get you home," he replied, smiling mischievously.

We managed to get the rest of my clothes on without any more foul play, and by the time we finished, the doctor was back with news that I could leave. When Big lifted me off the bed, I thought that he intended to put me back in the wheelchair, but instead, he cradled me to his chest and carried me out front to a waiting 2019 candy apply red two door Rolls Royce Phantom.

"What did you do, trade in the car that I bought you?" I asked.

"No, I just bought you one to match."

I made sure to give him a juicy kiss for his love and consideration before he put me in the passenger seat.

"I'm assuming it's bulletproof," I said once he'd gotten behind the wheel and pulled off.

"You damn right. Like Yo Gotti said, we gangsta, but we ain't bulletproof."

"It seems like you've been real busy while I was asleep," I said.

"I had to do everything in my power not to lose my mind, babe, because the thought of life without you was torture," he admitted.

I took his hand in mine and kissed his fingers, wishing that I could put into words how much I loved him. The smile on his face told me that he understood though. I closed my eyes and leaned my head back against the soft Italian leather, wanting to bask in all that was good while organizing my thoughts around all the bad that was to come. I would embrace both things because they were needed in my life. I'd learned from my dad a long time ago that you couldn't have the good without the bad.

"Now what?" Big said in frustration.

I opened my eyes to see what had caused his statement, noticing that we were home already.

"Who is that?" I asked.

"That's Juanito standing by the truck, but I don't know who that is climbing out the back."

"That's Manuel," I said.

My first question was why they were here. My next question was why they were here with their guns out.

"Did you call them?" I asked.

"No."

"Do you have a gun on you?" I asked.

The sound of him chambering a bullet was his answer.

Chapter 5
Ebony

"You don't seriously believe that your own sister would betray you for *Ivy*, do you?" I asked skeptically.

"On the contrary. I think that Ivy is the only person that she'd do some shit like that for. They were close once upon a time, maybe close enough for Darlise to tell her the truth about me."

"And what truth would that be?" I asked.

For a second he looked at me, but I could tell that he wasn't actually seeing me. When his eyes swam back into focus, they brought that same coldness with them that signified his mind being on some other shit.

"Darlise's mom told her that I'd killed her dad for no reason," he replied.

"Okay…but you didn't, right?"

"No, I killed him for a good reason. His ass *needed* killing," Justice said seriously.

I wouldn't open my mouth and speak my judgment because I lived in a glass house, but I was damn sure judging him in my mind.

"I'm assuming that this happened a long time ago, so why do you think that she would all of a sudden betray you now? And who told you this shit anyway?" I asked.

"The information is reliable because I've got a man inside Big's line-up that feeds me info when he can. It makes perfect sense too because I had no idea that my sister was in Texas or that she was seeing Ivy, and when I asked why she'd shot her, she told me that she thought Ivy was there to kill her. At the time I thought that was possible if Ivy had found out what my play was in the port, and it was obvious that she did find out because of the drive-by. The only problem is that my sister should've been at school in South Carolina, not in Texas. As for the timing of her betrayal, that's simple. This was really the first opportunity she had to hurt me."

"Maybe, but that was her nephew that got killed," I reminded him gently.

"I think that's why she killed Ivy, because him getting hurt wasn't part of the plan. I'm not even sure that it was part of Ivy's plan, because it would've made more sense to use my son to get to me. I mean, she'd played it smart up until that point by not letting on that she knew what I was up to, so the drive-by was stupid."

"So why did she do it?" I asked, confused.

"I don't know how many times I've asked myself that same question since it happened, and the only answer I can see is that somebody's wires got crossed somewhere."

Hearing this brought an alien feeling of guilt up inside me. True enough, I'd killed Ivy's dad because she'd killed mine, but I'd done it at that particular time because Ivy had killed Justice's son. I'd wanted to take from her like she'd been taking from other people, but now it was sounding like the responsibility wasn't all hers.

"So now what?" I asked.

Before he could answer, the fasten seatbelt light dinged on, alerting us that we were about to land. We both moved from the couch back to our seats and we buckled up. Suddenly, my apprehension about being back wasn't simply about the ongoing war because it was obvious that no one could be trusted at this point. It was impossible to sleep with both eyes open.

Ten minutes later, we touched down in Oakland, and it was officially too late to turn back.

"Is someone meeting us?" I asked.

"Yeah."

Based on his nonchalant response to that question, I'd expected a couple of his homies to meet us outside the terminal, but when we got out front, there were five black Escalades waiting. No one was actually standing outside waiting for us, but I had no doubt that was because everybody had a gun of some sort. We climbed into the back of the second SUV, and moments later, our caravan was on the move.

"Where are we going?" I asked.

"I'm taking you to a safe place, and then I've got some business to handle."

It wasn't hard to conclude that the business that he had to handle was pertaining to his sister, which meant it was important, but even knowing that didn't make me feel comfortable being without him.

"I'm not going somewhere without you," I said.

"You're good with my people, EB, they'll protect you."

"I understand what you're saying, but you're obviously not hearing me," I persisted.

When he cut his eyes in my direction, I could see the single-minded focus that he was under, but if I let him get away with putting anything ahead of mine and my baby's safety now, then he'd do it at the wrong time in the future.

"You sure you wanna go with me? This shit might get ugly," he warned seriously.

"No offense to your homies, but I feel safer by your side, no matter what's going on."

He nodded his head in understanding before leaning forward and whispering something to the two men in the front seat. When he sat back, I took his hand in mine and gave it a gentle squeeze in thanks. He smiled at me, but neither of us spoke again until we pulled up to a little house on a quiet street in a neighborhood in desperate need of revitalizing.

"I think you should wait out here," he stated.

Up until this point I'd had my doubts about his ability to actually hurt his sister, but the way he'd made this statement gave me chills and made me question what I thought I knew. Still, I didn't turn his hand loose or look away from his unwavering gaze. After a few minutes, he nodded his head in acceptance and we climbed out of the SUV. My assumption about why nobody had been standing outside their rides when we came out of the airport was proven true because when my feet hit the sidewalk, we were suddenly surrounded by at least thirty armed men.

"Damn," I mumbled under my breath.

"I want the house surrounded," Justice said, leading the way to the front door.

The men quickly spread out, but my focus was on keeping up with Justice's purposeful strides. When he got to the front door he knocked like this was a normal house call, even answering calmly to the voice that called out to ask who it was. When the door opened, there was a short brown-skinned woman standing there, but Justice's swift jab pushed her back inside the house while sliding her across the floor. I could see a muscular dark-skinned nigga hop up off the couch, but before he could advance, one of Justice's homies moved past both of us with a pistol leveled at him. The nigga was smart enough not to move, but it was clear to see that he most definitely wanted to.

"J-justice, what the fuck?!" Darlise yelled from her spot on the floor.

In response, Justice crossed to where she was, grabbed her hair, and lifted her to her feet. I could tell that Darlise was opening her mouth to plead with her brother, but he fired a right hook that damn near broke her neck. Instantly she was unconscious, and she was only remaining upright because of the grip Justice had on her hair.

"Put her in the truck," Justice ordered, taking the gun out of his homie's hand in exchange for Darlise.

"Yo, Justice, what the fuck, bruh? I - "

Whatever the nigga still standing by the couch was gonna say was permanently frozen when Justice put a nice hole in his forehead, dropping him.

"Let's go," he said, turning around, taking my hand, and leading the way back out to the Escalade.

Within a couple of minutes we were on the move again, almost as if that brief stop had been a figment of my imagination. The gun resting in Justice's lap told me that I hadn't dreamed any of what had just happened, which meant shit was definitely destined to get worse. I wasn't sure what I should say, but I felt the need to say *something*.

"J, I know she fucked up, but - "

"She didn't fuck up. She got my son killed. That's not forgivable," he said calmly.

He wasn't looking at me, but I knew what his eyes were showing the world, just like I knew that there was no way to talk him out of whatever he had planned. Right about now I was wishing that I'd listened to him when he'd insisted that I be somewhere besides in this moment, but I *was* here, and something told me that it was too late to turn back.

We rode in silence for another fifteen minutes before pulling up to a house similar in construction and location. This time when we got out, Justice didn't have to give orders because half the men were leading the way into the house while the rest posted up to monitor the dark street. It was obvious to me that this was the base of operations - at least for the moment.

"You hungry?" Justice asked once we'd made it inside.

"A little."

"What do you want to eat?" he asked.

"I don't know. I'm not really having cravings yet. I did work up an appetite on the plane though," I replied, smirking at him.

I could tell that he had to fight to suppress his smile.

"Why don't you look in the kitchen and see if anything calls out to you? It's fully stocked."

I knew that he was probably concerned with making sure I ate and stayed healthy for the baby's sake, but I also knew that he was trying to distract me from whatever he was about to do. I kissed him softly on the cheek before making my way to the kitchen at the back of the house.

It was immediately clear to see that the word stocked was an understatement because there was food stacked on every counter. When I opened the refrigerator, I found more of the same, but I decided to simply make a sandwich. I took everything out that I needed to the little table in the corner of the kitchen, but before I could get started, a blood-chilling scream ripped through the night. I knew who the scream belonged to and that she earned whatever was happening, but it was still unsettling. The sounds were coming from the backyard, and the crisp night air was carrying everything to me like surround sound, which made me feel like I was in the middle of the action. In between the screams I could hear uncontrollable crying and begging, but the scariest part was that those were the only sounds I heard. Not once had I heard anyone speak, not even Justice. My curiosity finally got the best of me, forcing me to set my sandwich down and go to the back door where I could see the entire backyard.

There was a crowd of people outside, and it probably would've been impossible to make out what was clearly going on in the moonlight, but someone had lit a fire. By the fires glow I could see that Darlise was naked and bent backwards over an oil drum with her wrists handcuffed to her ankles. The angle that she was bent at was no doubt painful, especially with that hard metal digging into her, back, but I knew that wasn't what had her screaming. I watched in fascinated horror as Justice pulled the small shovel one would use for a fireplace out of the flames, and pressed it down on the bare flesh of his sister's stomach. Even though it was impossible, I could swear that I heard her skin sizzle like bacon in a pan of hot grease. The screams she let loose had me convinced of just how painful it was too. My eyes quickly darted around to the neighboring house, fearing that someone would overhear and call the police, but I knew Justice wouldn't be doing this here unless it was safe.

When I refocused my attention back to what was going on, I saw that the shovel was back inside the fire, and Justice was now whispering something in Darlise's ear. Only they knew what was being said, but I could clearly read the expression on her face. Hopelessness. I knew in that moment that Justice hadn't run down on his sister to question her about what he'd been told because in his heart, he believed it to be true. Which meant it didn't matter if it *wasn't* true. Darlise was still gonna die tonight.

I wanted to turn away and go back to my sandwich, but my feet were rooted to their current position and my eyes refused to look away. I don't know how long I stood in that one spot, but it was long enough to watch Justice burn and brand every part of her body and for her constant screams to simply become background noise in my mind. When he didn't put the shovel back in the fire, I assumed that he was done, and that he would now put the bullet in her that would end her existence.

I was wrong. He stepped to the side of her, making me think that he was gonna talk to her again, but instead, he cocked the shovel back and swung mightily. The sound of the warm metal contacting with Darlise's face was a sickening splat that echoed across the small backyard. It was unclear to me when she lost consciousness versus when she actually died because he just kept hitting her over and over again. When he finally ran out of energy, he dropped the shovel and spit on the now-unrecognizable Darlise. I could hear someone saying something to him, but his focus was now on the back door - or more accurately, on me. I didn't know what he was looking for any more than I knew what my face was currently revealing, but it wasn't until he looked away that I was finally able to move. I sat back at the table, despite the thought of me eating being the furthest thing from my mind.

Being here, in this situation, wasn't what I'd seen for myself twenty-four hours ago, especially not with me being pregnant. A bullet had cost me my first child, but if I'd learned nothing else from watching Justice, I learned that there were different ways to die out here. My history with Justice was as complicated as my present, but J knew there was love there. The problem was that he'd just demonstrated that love and good intentions weren't enough of a reason not to kill you. Naturally the questions running through my mind were what would happen if I suddenly found myself on his bad side…and what if this baby wasn't his?

"You okay?" Justice asked, coming in through the back door and crossing to the sink to wash his hands.

"I'm fine. Are you okay?"

"I don't know that I'll ever be okay. I'm simply living life moment to moment," he confused.

"That's all that we can do, I guess."

When he turned around to face me, I picked up my sandwich in order to busy my hands and hide my nervousness. The turkey tasted like cardboard going down, but I forced myself to eat at a normal rate while seeing the man I'd shared an emotional connection with on the plane instead of his utter ego.

"How much did you see?" he asked finally.

"Not a lot, it was dark. I heard her though," I replied, telling a half truth.

"You probably think I'm a monster, huh?"

"No, I think you're grieving, and you have a right to do that," I said, deflecting what he was really getting at with another lie.

"I am grieving, but I don't want you to think that takes my focus away from you and the baby, because it doesn't."

"Justice, that never crossed my mind."

"Good, because I plan on us being a family, and nothing is more important than family."

Aryanna

Chapter 6
Ivy

"Manuel, I didn't expect you to come all the way out here to welcome me home," I said, closing the door to my car and watching the two men in front of me closely.

"This is a happy coincidence, I assure you," Manuel replied, looking at Big, who was still sitting in the car.

"Really? So is your visit business or pleasure?" I asked curiously.

"Business. We wanted to talk to Big about - "

"Well, if you're here about business, Juanito, then you can talk to me," I said, giving my friendliest smile.

Despite my calm, I knew that these men weren't fools, so they knew that I felt some type of way about them showing up at my house with their guns drawn. I wouldn't address that elephant in the room just yet though.

"Big has been running things while you were in the hospital, but not how you would've run it," Juanito replied.

"That's because we're two different people. I know without a doubt that Big would only make rational, logical decisions though. So what's the problem?" I asked.

"The problem is that he hasn't made good on the promises that you made about our distribution once Sinola was out of the picture," Manuel said, still looking at Big.

"Ah, I see why that might upset you. Do you know what upsets me? Getting shot twice because of your fuck up," I replied, no longer smiling.

It could've been my tone that forced the men in front of me to swing their eyes in my direction, or it could've been the pistol in my hand that I'd pulled from behind my back. Either way, I now had their attention.

"I don't appreciate your tone," Manuel stated.

"And I don't appreciate you showing up at my house with your hitta in tow like you're about to do something to my man," I replied.

The look in both men's eyes spoke of their willingness to kill, but the sound of a gun being cocked behind them still caused both of them to flinch slightly.

"Well then, why don't we go sit down like civilized folk and discuss what needs to be done," I suggested.

The two men exchanged a look that I wouldn't have called defeat as much as recalculation. It was obvious that they'd come here with the intention of intimidation, and I'd suspected as much, which was why I'd made Big let me handle it. They don't know my nigga like I did because if they did, then they never would've dreamed of trying this move. Big was with all the bullshit that the streets were made of, and not even the infamous powers of the cartel could put fear in his heart. I respected that about him, but I wasn't willing to let him risk his life to prove what a bad mu'fucka he was. There was more than one way to skin a cat. The fact that my business partners tucked their weapons back inside their expensive suits signaled that they understood this philosophy too. I nodded at James, and he lowered the two guns he'd been pointing at the back of Juanito's and Manuel's heads. When Big went to pick me up, I started to stop him because I didn't want to appear fragile in front of anyone, but I owed it to my man to put my pride away and let him take care of me. Once I was engulfed in the safety of his arms, he carried me into the living room and put me on the white leather loveseat, taking a seat beside me. Juanito and Manuel sat across from us on the couch, and James hovered nearby.

"Alright, gentlemen, what's the problem?" I asked.

"There's been no movement in a week, and our various distributers throughout the U.S. aren't happy about that," Manuel said.

"My woman got shot and has been in a coma. Do you think I'm happy about that?" Big asked with barely restrained hostility.

"Have we not been lending all of our support in an effort to eliminate those responsible for what happened?" Juanito countered.

I knew that the next thing to come out of Big's mouth was that all this shit was their fault anyway, and I knew that having that argument was counterproductive.

"I appreciate your willingness to go to war on my behalf. I'm sure that you can understand that with everything going on, business just kinda fell through the cracks," I said.

"We do understand that you have been through a great deal," Manuel replied.

Even though he didn't say it, everyone in the room heard the "but" at the end of his sentence.

"Now that I'm home, I'm sure that we can have your shipment in the water by morning, provided that it's ready to move from your end," I stated.

"It's ready for transport," Manuel replied.

"Good. Is there anything else that we need to discuss?" Big asked.

Again Juanito and Manuel exchanged a look, but this one wasn't as easily transparent as the last.

"Have you made any progress in your search for the one who killed Soloman?" Manuel asked.

"Yes and no," Big replied vaguely.

"What does that mean?" Juanito asked.

"It means that my people are making progress, but I don't have that bitch's head on my trophy wall yet," Big said.

"Okay, well, keep me posted."

"I know that you want her dead, but it's sometimes hard to catch someone who's running for their life because they're extremely desperate. Someone like Justice is more problematic, though, because he's not running. He's standing his ground and willing to die as long as he can take somebody with him," Juanito stated.

Right away, I saw what he was getting at.

"So you think it's a wiser decision to focus more on Justice, and less on Ebony, at this moment?" I asked, nodding my head.

"It makes sense because one has an army, and one doesn't," Manuel replied simply.

"That probably would've been a good suggestion last week, but the last update that I get makes me believe that Justice and Ebony are now together," Big said.

This piece of information caused Juanito and Manuel to huddle together and whisper amongst themselves. After a few moments, they turned their attention back on us.

"Do you know where they are?" Juanito asked.

"Not yet, but I should have a general location soon," Big replied.

"We might be able to use the same tactic that we used to get to Esteban," Manuel said.

"Okay," I said, waiting for an explanation.

"The way we got to Esteban was through a drone strike that levelled his entire compound," Juanito informed us.

When I looked at Big, I found him looking back at me with the same expression of being impressed covering his face.

"Well, that's one way to do it," I replied, chuckling.

"There will be a lot of casualties, but it's effective," Manuel said.

"What if we had a different way to go after Ebony, while focusing all of our street resources on the war with Justice?" I asked.

"I'm listening," Manuel replied.

"I have in my possession a video recording of Ebony killing Esteban's nephew, the one that the Sinola Cartel sent to kill her mother. Despite who the victim is, that recording would still bring the weight of law enforcement down on her," I said.

"It would also bring the Sinola Cartel out too, even though they would never agree to work with us," Juanito stated thoughtfully.

I could tell by the look in Manuel's eyes that he was giving my idea careful consideration, which was a good sign. The situation that Rockafella had put himself in when he tried to frame Big for a cold case had taught me the importance of conferring with your business partners before pulling a move that involved the police. Good intentions didn't count for shit in the art of war. Only making the right move at the right time mattered.

"Videos can be faked or doctored, which makes them hardly reliable enough for the authorities to apply the pressure that you're envisioning," Manuel stated.

"That may be true, but we've still got the body, and the gun with Ebony's prints on it," Big said, smiling.

This setup had been well thought out and in motion long before Ebony stepped foot onto our childhood field of dreams and killed a man. Big and I had both agreed that giving Ebony blind trust was dumb as shit, so we'd devised an insurance plan to make sure that bitch *never* got away scot free.

"So you're saying that you've got Ebony for first degree murder?" Juanito asked.

"That's *exactly* what I'm saying," I replied, smiling slightly.

"Well played," Manuel said with admiration in his tone to match the look on his face.

"Indeed," Juanito chimed in.

"I'm sure that you can understand why we don't proceed with this plan without consulting with you first," I replied, playing to their sense of importance.

"I appreciate that consideration. It shows wisdom beyond your years," Manuel said genuinely.

"If you'll provide me with a copy of the recording, I know how to get it to the Sinaloa Cartel," Juanito stated.

I nodded to Big, who in turn stood up and escorted Juanito from the room, which left me, James, and Manuel alone. Manuel and I knew what needed to happen right now, but I knew that it wasn't easy for a man who was used to doing things his way. I also knew that he was intelligent enough to understand the harm he'd done to his business relationship with me by showing up at my house like he had. There was no way for Manuel and the Gulf Cartel to hold onto what they'd taken from the Sinola Cartel without the lanes of distribution that I offered. Therefore, he needed me, and we both knew that.

"Ivy, I must apologize for being so hot-headed earlier. I know that you're a woman of your word, and in this business, that is as important as money. I will keep that in mind for the future," he said contritely.

"I appreciate your apology, Manuel. I know that having your bottom line affected is unacceptable when you have so many subordinates depending on you for their survival. It's my hope that once we get this thing going, it'll run smoothly enough to continue while our attention is focused on other business."

"I'm sure that it will, especially with the new strategy you're about to deploy. What are your plans after that?" he asked.

"Well, since no one knows that I'm still alive, I plan to remain here away from prying eyes. I trust that you can keep my miracle resurrection between us," I replied, giving him a knowing smile.

"Of course."

For some reason, it had been on the tip of my tongue to tell him that I was pregnant, but I quickly squashed that urge. I know that men like him already felt that women had a specific position and role in life because we were the weaker, and inferior sex, so I wasn't about to reveal anything that would alter the level of respect that I'd demanded thus far. Besides, news of my baby only needed to be shared with those who could appreciate the blessing that it was. Big's and Juanito's sudden reappearance effectively ended our private conversation anyway.

"The quality is quite good," Juanito conceded, passing his phone to Manuel.

We all watched in silence as Manuel watched Ebony empty the clip into Esteban's favorite nephew.

"I'd say that this will certainly reinvigorate Esteban's family, especially since it gives them an enemy to go after that they can actually defeat," Manuel said.

"When will you get it to them?" Big asked.

"As soon as possible. When will you turn it over to the police?" Juanito asked.

"I'm thinking that we should wait a couple weeks to see if we can resolve it to our satisfaction first, because once the cops are involved, it'll make it harder for your men in the street," I replied.

"And in the meantime, I'll work on locating her and coordinating with you, Juanito, so that we have our ground forces moving together," Big said.

"It sounds like we have a plan then. I'll contact you shortly about moving a shipment," Manuel said, extending his hand for me to shake.

We all shook hands before James escorted them out, leaving Big and me in the living room.

"That went better than I thought it would when we pulled up," I said, laying back into the softness of the couches cushions.

Big's response was an inaudible grunt that conveyed clearly his unhappiness about not being allowed to make a meal out of our unexpected guests.

"Believe it or not, Manuel did apologize," I said, looking over at him.

"Juanito did too."

"Then don't let that shit bother you, babe, because we've got bigger shit to worry about. I do appreciate you letting me handle it, though, because I know how hard that was for you," I acknowledged.

"You're welcome, baby. You know I'd do anything for you," he replied, taking my hand in his.

He'd definitely proven the truth of that statement, and I loved him more for it.

"As soon as I'm well enough, I'ma put this pussy on you righteously, I promise."

"When you get well enough? Oh nah, bae, I'm sleeping in that pussy tonight," he replied, smiling devilishly.

"No you not either. You know that I can't keep up with you right now."

"I guess that means you're just gonna have to become a slave to this dick then," he said, smiling wider.

I wanted to hit him because I knew that he meant exactly what he said, but I was too weak for that, so I settled for blowing him a kiss with my middle finger. Of course this only made him laugh out loud as he leaned over to kiss me. The passion that he ignited with the simple touch of his lips to mine had me seeing visions on the back of my eyelids of me getting dicked down right here on the couch. Hearing James come back into the room put all those thoughts on hold though, as the next pressing matter of business surfaced in my mind.

"Who's working the front gate, James?" I asked calmly.

"That would be Ryan and Jonesy," he replied.

"Bring them up here," I demanded.

He immediately turned and left.

"What's up, baby?" Big asked.

"I just want to make sure they know not to let people in who ain't on the list. Pass me your guns," I replied, holding my hand out.

I could feel his reluctance, but he still did as I asked and put the Glock .27 in my palm. Looking at the gun in my hand made me think of my father, and my chest suddenly got tight.

"My-my dad's funeral - "

"It was beautiful, I promise. I would've waited to do it, but no one could tell me when or if you would wake up," Big said softly.

"I'm glad you took care of everything because it would've been too hard for me to deal with. Thank you."

We both remembered how hard my mom's funeral had been for me emotionally, and that was *before* Ebony and Rock had shot the service up. Thinking about that now made me wish that I'd killed both of their mu'fucking asses when I had the chance, but I knew that for Ebony, the opportunity would present itself again. And I wouldn't hesitate.

When the three men entered the room, I could feel the fear and nervousness hovering around all of them. I took my time ejecting the clip from the pistol and checking it before slamming it back in and pulling the slide back.

"The two men waiting in my driveway. Were they on the approved list?" I asked calmly.

Ryan and Jonesy looked at each other, but no one volunteered to speak first.

"Based on your silence, I'll assume that your answer is no. I can't stress with words how unacceptable it is to let someone near my home, but hopefully my actions will convey what I'm saying." I stated.

I quickly fired four shots, giving the two men an equal amount of hot slugs in their chest.

"James, do I have to explain to you how serious I am?" I asked.

"No, Ms. Black, I understand."

"Good. Please dispose of the bodies," I requested.

"Now what?" Big asked.

"Now we exchange vows - unless you've changed your mind," I replied.

He looked from me to the gun in my hand, and back.

"No, I'm yours for life."

Chapter 7
Ebony
One month later

"Oh-ohhh shit!" I moaned loudly, riding Justice faster.

I could tell by the way that he was bucking beneath me that he was moments away from catching the same ghost that I was chasing. We definitely made a hell of a team, and before I knew it, his upward thrusts combined with my downward force shattered my world like fine china against a wall. Within seconds of my climax, I felt the heat of his cum invade me with the force of a battle battalion as a strangled growl leapt from his throat. The death grip that he had on my hips forced me to slow all the way down, but I kept riding him until the last of the orgasmic tremors had stopped causing me to see sparkles everywhere I looked. The air from the open window caused the sweat on my skin to cool rapidly, but instead of snuggling up with Justice for warmth, I climbed off of him and went into the bathroom to take a shower.

For the first five minutes under the heat and power of the water's spray, my body remained tense and rigid, but once I realized that he wasn't coming to join me, I relaxed. I was able to let my guard all the way down, and like normal, that's when the tears came. I clamped my hands tightly over my mouth as I collapsed to the floor and gave into the sobs that rocked my body harder than any orgasm could. The first time this had happened I'd been terrified because I couldn't understand why I was crying, and I'd almost been hysterical that first time around. Sex with Justice wasn't forced. It was a choice that I made each and every time to fulfill my body's needs. But emotionally, it always left me in this same position. By my second episode of crying, I'd figured out why. It was Rockafella. To say that I missed him wasn't nearly a strong enough statement, and the guilt I felt every time that I fucked a nigga that wasn't him was enough to drown me in my own tears. So many times in the course of a day I asked myself if this was really my life, or if it was a nightmare that I'd wake up from soon? Somehow I felt like I wouldn't get that answer until it was too late.

I spent a solid ten minutes on the floor crying my eyes out before finally getting up and bathing myself. Despite the hot shower and the emotional cleansing that came from shedding tears, I still didn't feel any better about my life's trajectory. In the last thirty days, I'd lived differently than my previous twenty-three years of life. Because we had to keep a low profile, having money did me no good right now. That meant I'd had to move from project house to project house, sometimes in the middle of the night, and I had to live like anybody else who was on the run. I'd imagined what Justice had to be going through fighting the Hoovers and the cartel, but actually living life with him made it clear that what I'd thought hadn't come close to being accurate. To him, every day was the same and survival was his focus, but I wanted to live. I didn't see how that was possible in this situation, or without Rock by my side. Justice was a good dude, and I felt like he would keep me safe to the best of his abilities. He wasn't an adequate substitute for Rockafella though. No one was.

I got out of the shower and dried off before returning to the bedroom that we'd been sharing for the last four days. Most nights I slept alone because Justice had business to handle, but surprisingly, that didn't bother me nearly as much as it had that first night we'd arrived in Oakland. He'd given me my pick of handguns to protect myself with, and so my Glock .23 with an extended hundred round drum gave me the safety that I needed.

"Hungry?" he asked when I came into the room.

"No."

"You know how important it is to eat," he stated, while diligently rolling a blunt.

"Yeah, I know," I replied, with mounting frustration as I grabbed something to wear out of the duffle bag I was living out of.

"So what do you want to eat then?"

"I'm not hungry, Justice, and if I was, then I know how to find my way to the kitchen," I stated, losing the battle with my annoyance.

For a few moments he didn't say anything, which allowed me to get dressed in peace, but the smell of weed burning told me that his silence had only been because his attention was momentarily diverted. He hadn't let the topic go, and he wouldn't, because it directly tied to the baby I was carrying.

"I don't want to fight with you, Justice," I said, turning to face him.

"That's good because I don't want that either, but - "

"But I need to eat, I know, I heard you the first time," I said.

"Actually, I was gonna say that I know you need to get out, so why don't I take you out to eat?"

"Out? You mean like to McDonald's or something?" I asked unenthusiastically.

"No, I mean out as in a restaurant where I'm required to tip the waiter," he replied, smiling and blowing smoke at the ceiling.

"F-for real?"

"I can tell by the tone of your voice and the look on your face that you're surprised, but yeah, I'm being serious. I know that this past month has been hard on you, probably harder than anything you've ever been through in some ways, and I hate that because I never wanted this life for you. This isn't my way of punishing you though, sweetheart. I simply don't trust your safety to anyone else except me," he replied.

"I never thought that you were punishing me. I just wasn't mentally prepared to deal with this," I confessed.

"I don't think anyone who didn't grow up like this is mentally prepared to deal with it from the jump. Being in a constant war zone ain't something that you can prepare for until you've gone through it, and survived to remember it."

"Will we survive this, J?" I asked, looking at him closely.

"You should know by now that I'm too stubborn for there to be any other outcome except our victory."

I chose to acknowledge the truth in his answer instead of the cockiness because I knew just how stubborn and determined he was. Neither of these things guaranteed victory, but they provided some comfort.

"So where were you thinking of taking me to eat?" I asked.

"That all depends on what you've got a taste for."

The smirk on his face made his choice clear, but I just shook my head because as of yet, I hadn't sucked his dick, and I didn't know when or if I would. I didn't mind him eating my pussy, but I wasn't ready to give myself completely to him - or anybody else, for that matter.

"Are there any good soul food places out here?" I asked.

"Say no more. I know where to take you, and you don't even gotta change clothes."

His mentioning my attire had me looking down self-consciously at the stonewashed jeans and plain white T-shirt that I had on. I could remember a time not too long ago when Ivy had taken me to her house and insisted that I get all dressed up because the Ebony that *she* knew always looked on point. My Gucci dresses and Fendi bags seemed like memories from a lifetime ago, and I knew that thinking about who I was wouldn't help me right now.

"Well, if I don't gotta change then I guess I'm waiting on you," I said.

He got out of the bed and passed me the rest of the blunt before going to take a quick shower. Normally I only smoked when I first woke up because weed had proven to deal with my morning sickness, but since I had time to kill, I sat on the bed and indulged. When Justice emerged from the bathroom fifteen minutes later I was flat on my back, looking at the imaginary clouds moving across the chipped paint on the ceiling.

"Seeing you like that gives me other ideas besides going out to eat," he said.

"No more pussy until you feed me."

"Yeah, it definitely sounds like you're hungry now," he replied, laughing.

It only took him a couple minutes to get dressed, and then we were ready to go.

"You got your gun?" he asked before we left the room.

I pointed at the purse swinging from my left arm. Satisfied, he led the way downstairs, where he picked out enough niggas to fill up the two SUV's that would be escorting us on our travels. Within a few minutes, we were all loaded up and moving through the city.

"So how are things going?" I asked, looking out the window and thinking about the day I could once again walk around like a normal person.

"Pretty much the same as it has been. We're trading bodies," he replied.

Hearing this was depressing, not because of the senseless loss of life, but because if there was no progress being made, then there was no ending in sight for this cage I now lived in.

"If this ain't settled by the time you're six months pregnant, then I'm gonna have to try something different," he said.

"Like what?"

"Like leaving - at least until after the baby is born," he replied.

I turned to look at him, not knowing what expression I would find on his face, but pleasantly surprised by the serious look that he was giving me.

"You're for real? You'd really leave Oakland for an extended period of time?" I asked.

"Ebony, I hope that I haven't given you the impression that this war is more important than you or our baby because it's not. Survival for *all* of us is the most important thing, and I'd do whatever I had to in order to ensure that."

"I know that. I also know how loyal you are," I said.

"True, but I already had the necessary conversations with my homies. So if we gotta leave, we're gone."

Hearing this helped me breathe a little easier, especially since I was almost three months pregnant now. It shouldn't have surprised me that Justice would put us first, but it kinda did. He was the quintessential street nigga, which meant that when it was his time to go, he'd wanna die on the same block that he'd repped his entire life. Understanding that told me exactly how hard the decision to leave had been for him, and I respected him more for it.

I took his hand in mine, and smiled at him with genuine gratitude. The smile that he gave in return was full of love, and it made me feel guilty. Deep down I knew that I'd always loved him, and I always would on some level, but my heart still belonged to Rockafella. Shifting my gaze back out of the window to the passing scenery, I once again asked myself what would happen if Justice wasn't my baby's daddy. True enough, I had slept with him without using protection, but something inside me was telling me that this baby was Rock's. Despite my emotional instability, I was still able to acknowledge that this could've been nothing more than wishful thinking on my part, but I didn't think it was. I'd bet my life that I was carrying Rock's baby, and I had no idea how Justice would react to that news.

"Have you thought about baby names yet?" he asked suddenly.

Of course I had. What pregnant woman didn't? But I knew that this couldn't be my reply.

"No, not really. I wanted to wait until I was further along," I lied.

"Well, you already know what it has to be if it's a boy."

I wanted to tell him that he had absolutely no say in what I decided to name my child, but instead, I kept my gaze focused out the window.

"You don't have a problem with that, do you?" he asked when I didn't respond.

"Huh? I'm sorry, I was just thinking about my dad. When I was pregnant before, I'd thought about naming the baby after him."

I didn't even have to look at Justice to know that whatever argument he'd been about to put forth about my child carrying his name was now swallowed - at least for the moment. We rode on in silence, and I was more than okay with that as my thoughts moved on into the uncertain future that awaited. One thing that I knew for sure was that I had too many unaccomplished dreams to waste a single moment once things get back to normal.

"We're here," Justice announced, letting my hand go.

When the SUV came to a stop we both got out and made our way inside of Big Mama's soul food restaurant. The building wasn't much to look at from the outside, but on the inside, it smelled like home. The familiar aromas of southern home cooking invoked a nostalgia in me that put tears in my eyes, but I refused to cry right now. Instead, I tried to focus on what I would eat first. We were led to a corner booth, and once we sat down, our drink orders were taken.

"Thank you for bringing me here, J," I said.

"You're welcome. I won't lie to you and say that the food is better than your mom's, but that's only because your mom's food was perfect. It's still good eating though."

"I hope you brought your wallet then, because me and this baby are getting ready to *grease*," I stated emphatically.

Before Justice could respond, two men stopped at our table, and the immediate change in the atmosphere was easy to feel.

"You lost, cuz?" one man asked.

"He damn sure must be lost," the other man said.

"This is neutral territory. I'm not looking for any problems," Justice replied calmly.

"Ain't no such thing as neutral territory, and you're wearing the wrong colors to be in this neighborhood. I'll tell you what though. Since you don't want no problems, all you gotta do is come up out of those shoes and we'll be on our way," the first man stated.

I wasn't a hood bitch from the street, but I knew enough to know that this was some typical gang shit going on. The shoes that Justice had on weren't special. They were only Converse. They were red though, and if he surrendered them to those two niggas that I presumed were Crips, it would have a lasting effect on things that I couldn't comprehend.

My eyes darted around the restaurant, hoping to find at least one of Justice's homies inside with us, but from the looks of things, everybody was waiting in the parking lot. And why wouldn't they be if this was thought to be a safe location? All I knew was that that assumption was about to cost us.

Justice didn't respond verbally to the demand made, but instead, he smiled at the two men. Apparently that was the wrong thing to do, though, because suddenly pistols came out and they were attacking Justice with them. I reacted by instinct, pulling the gun from my purse and dumping two shots into both of the men hitting Justice. They immediately dropped, and when I spotted movement out of my peripheral vision, I swung my gun to the left and pulled the trigger again. The man I'd shot in the face had been holding a gun in his right hand, which made him a threat, but he was holding something worse in his left hand. A badge. I didn't have time to think about what I'd done before Justice was pulling me out of the restaurant and pushing me into the back of the SUV.

"Drive!" he demanded angrily.

"J-Justice, I-I shot - "

"Yeah, I saw. You saved my life, but it looks like we're leaving sooner than I thought. They take cop killing serious out here."

Chapter 8
Ivy

"Baby? Bae? Ivy, you didn't hear me calling you?"

"Huh?" I replied distractedly, looking at Big coming down the hallway.

Before he got to my side, my eyes were once again focused on what had been occupying my attention for at least the last ten minutes.

"You okay?" Big asked gently.

I gave a slight nod while continuing to stare at the empty bed in front of me. The last time I'd stepped foot in this room my father had been lying in that bed, and the fact that he wasn't now made it impossible to cross the door's threshold. I couldn't count how many times I'd stood in this exact same spot in the last month just staring at this same empty bed, whispering silent prayers in my mind that God would somehow bring him back. I couldn't explain the physical ache inside me to have my daddy back, not even to Big.

"Baby, we need to go," Big said softly, taking my hand in his.

"I know," I replied, still not moving.

I knew that we had a doctor's appointment for my first trimester check-up, but right now, that was just another reminder of one more thing that my dad would miss out on. I knew that Big had had whatever damage done to the room repaired so that I wouldn't have to face it, but it made it seem like my dad would be back any moment. He wouldn't though. I'd been granted that wish once before, and as much as I believed in God, I didn't think he'd give me the same miracle twice. After taking a calming breath, I turned away from the open door and led the way out front to my car.

"You want me to drive?" Big offered.

"Nah, I'm good. Besides, you've been driving my car more than me."

"I'm just paying you back for how you did me when you first gave me my car," he replied, smiling at me.

"Uh huh, whatever. Plant your ass in that passenger seat and enjoy the ride."

Once I slid behind the wheel and started the car, I had to wait for Big's homies to load up in their Range Rovers, and then we moved out. Despite the fact of me still living and breathing remaining a secret thus far, Big wasn't taking any chances, and he'd made it perfectly clear that nothing that I said would change shit. I truthfully didn't mind all the security though, especially considering that we didn't have a fixed location on Ebony or Justice. All we knew was that her plane had touched down in Oakland, and that's where it stayed. I was beginning to think that Justice had built tunnels beneath Oakland because there hadn't been one sighting of him in three weeks! To say that I was frustrated was a serious understatement.

"You heard anything new yet?" I asked, hopeful.

"No, it's pretty much the same old shit with the only difference being the rise in the body count."

"Yeah, but it's not the *right* bodies," I said angrily.

"I know, bae. We'll get them though, and the fact that your business with Manuel is flourishing despite this war has Juanito and his people *very* motivated."

"I meant to mention that to you last night before we went to bed. Shit has been real quiet when it comes to the business, and ordinarily I'd say that a good thing, but Justice is too sneaky for my liking," I said.

"Okay…so what do you want me to do?" Big asked.

"I want you to change everything. Switch up the shipping and delivery schedules, and keep doing that every couple weeks so that we don't become predictable. I want you to move our personnel around too so we don't let anybody get too comfortable in their position, because then they might think that they're indispensable. I don't want them to feel like they've done anything wrong though, so make sure that everybody gets a bonus."

"How much?" he asked, already tapping his phones screen rapidly.

"Give everybody twenty thousand dollars, and tell them that it's in appreciation of their hard work. Lastly, I want anyone who's had something negative to say, or who's voiced criticism about our business practices from within our companies, gathered together. Make it seem like they've won a vacation, and then have then arrive at a specific place at a specific date and time."

"And then what?" he asked, looking at me.

We both knew that I didn't need to spell out the fact that those who couldn't be trusted had to die. I would no longer be giving some undeserving mu'fucka the benefit of doubt. After a few moments, he went back to his phone, and I turned my attention back to driving.

When I pulled up at the doctor's office twenty minutes later he'd just given his phone a much-needed rest.

"I got the right people on top of everything," he said.

"Thank you, baby, I appreciate you handling all that."

"It's my pleasure. You just don't know how sexy you are when you're on your boss bitch shit. I never in my wildest dreams thought that you would adapt to the role that you have to play now, but sometimes it's hard to remember when you *weren't* running shit," he replied seriously.

I knew that I was blushing under his praise, but I didn't care, because his opinion mattered the most to me.

"Between you and my dad I learned a lot, so you shouldn't be surprised if I'm good at this because I had the best teachers."

He leaned over and kissed me passionately enough to make me believe that I was most definitely about to be late for my doctor's appointment.

"What are you doing?" he asked when he felt my fingers assaulting his zipper.

"You know what I'm doing."

"B-bae, you know we can't do that. You're about to be examined, and we don't know what the doctor might wanna check," he said.

I heard the words coming from his mouth, but the moment I had his hard dick in my hand, his eyes spelled out surrender in all capital letters.

"You sure you want to wait?" I asked seductively, squeezing his dick until it throbbed in my hand.

"N-no I'm not sure, but-but we should."

Truthfully, I didn't have any intention on breezing into my doctor's office smelling freshly fucked, but I owed Big untold hours of torture for everything that he'd done to me before I was fully healed. If you asked him, he'd say that I'd gotten enough payback, but that's because he assumed that I only wanted to get even. No, I wanted to get ahead. My hand found its way to the base of his shaft, and my grip tightened. When his breathing turned ragged, I leaned over and spit on the dick, using my hand to evenly lubricate it before I fell face first on that angry mu'fucka.

"Ohhh lord!" he hissed through clenched teeth.

I could hear the fight for control with every breath that he took, but my sole focus was on what I had in my mouth.

My trip down had been fast, and I took every inch that God had blessed him without a hiccup of hesitation, but I worked my way back up his shaft slowly. By the time I got to where I only had the head of his dick clamped in between my lips, I could feel his entire body trembling. Without warning, I catapulted him to the back of my throat again, but this time I set a fast pace rhythm of up and down that had him moaning incoherently. It only took two minutes to make him my bitch and have him saying my name as I swallowed every drop of his hot cum.

"Didn't I tell you to stop eating so much salt," I said, pulling back and checking my makeup in my rearview mirror.

"Uh huh," he replied weakly.

"Then you need to start listening, unless you want me to stop swallowing."

"O-okay b-baby," he stammered.

"Now fix yourself up before you make us late," I said, opening my door and stepping out.

I was barely able to hold my laughter in when Big slowly got out of the car, but when he tripped on the curb, I lost the fight with myself and immediately gave into the giggles.

"You-you think you're funny don't you?"

"Baby, I don't know what you're talking about, now come on," I replied, putting on my oversized black sunglasses and leading the way into the doctor's office.

I knew that my lame attempt at a disguise probably wouldn't fool anybody, but the truth was that nobody was looking for a dead woman. Plus the fact that my hair was now long altered my appearance dramatically. Still, I'd had to pay out a lot of money and favors to important people in the last month to keep my rise from the grave quiet. The cops didn't necessarily mind because they knew that as long as I was presumed dead, then nobody would be coming into their jurisdiction to kill me. The Feds, on the other hand, had a lot of questions, but they couldn't get past my lawyer to get to me. Hoover Slim had made the witness in Big's cold case vanish, so that chapter in his life was officially closed. Every business that we owned was running like clockwork and could withstand a complete audit by the IRS at any time. The last piece of the puzzle had been Big and I exchanging vows, which we'd quietly done three weeks ago. Now we were bulletproof as far as the law using anything to force my hand about revealing that I was still alive or who'd tried to kill me. They'd have all the answers they needed soon enough, though, because I was determined to make at least two deaths very public. When we actually made it inside the doctor's office, I was surprised to find it empty, and her receptionist waved us straight through into the back.

"I'm sorry we're late, Dr. Paddington, it's his fault," I said, nodding my head towards Big, who was still clearly in another world.

"It's fine. I cleared my entire day for you anyway," Dr. Paddington replied.

"Oh, that explains why the waiting room is empty," I said.

"Yep, you're my only patient today. After I examine you, I'm going home so that my husband can pamper me."

"Well, then let's get to it because I do not want to deprive you of some good quality time with your man," I replied, climbing up on the table.

We went through the routine questions about morning sickness and pain I felt, and any blood spotting I saw. Once that formality was done, she hooked me up to the ultrasound machine and let our baby's strong heartbeat ride the airwaves in the room. The smile on Big's face said it all and pushed aside any lingering doubt I had about his desire to be a father.

"Do you wanna know what you're having?" Dr. Paddington asked, looking back and forth between us.

Big looked at me to make the decision, but I really didn't know what to say.

"I mean, if you want to, I'm okay with it," I said, looking at Big.

"Yeah, I wanna know," he replied eagerly.

The doctor moved the wand around some more on my stomach, but honestly, I couldn't tell the difference in what we were seeing.

"Is that his…?" Big asked, pointing at the screen.

"No, that's *her* arm," Dr. Paddington replied, chuckling softly.

"A-a girl? We're having a girl?" I asked.

"Yep, you sure are," the Dr. confirmed.

I kinda expected Big to be slightly disappointed because I knew that every man wanted a boy, but the look in his eyes was one of pure joy.

"I'm gonna have a little princess," he declared.

"Oh Lord, she ain't even here yet and you're already ready to spoil her," I said, shaking my head.

"Trust me, sweetie, you're fighting a losing battle. Men act like they want boys because it's the macho tough thing, but in truth, they want a female thy can submit to without being judged for it," Dr. Paddington said.

The look of righteous indignation on Big's face made me laugh out loud. Everyone in the room knew that the doctor was telling the truth, and thankfully, my husband was smart enough not to argue when he was severely out-numbered by woman power. We finished the rest of the exam, got our picture and appointment card, and then we were out the door. Before I could climb back behind the wheel, Big scooped me up into his arms and spun me around and around. "Boy, quit playing before I lose my breakfast," I said, laughing.

"Thank you, baby. I mean that from the bottom of my heart. I know that we never really talked about kids, and you made this decision on your own, but I'm still so thank-ful for you and that baby growing inside you," he replied sincerely.

The tears in his eyes touched me as much as his words did. I kissed him softly on the lips, feeling a kaleidoscope of emotions rotate through me. Thankfully, the joy out-weighed the sorrow.

"You're welcome, baby, but if you really want to thank me, then just be the amazing father that I know you're ca-pable of being."

"I promise, Ivy, I swear on my life that I'll be every-thing to our daughter, just like Soloman was to you," he vowed passionately.

Of course he would know the exact thing to say to make me cry right now, but it still wasn't with sadness. I missed my daddy, but his death didn't erase all that he'd done and all the he'd meant to be. Big didn't put me on my feet until he'd thoroughly kissed the path of my tears, which only made me want to cry harder, but I tucked those raw emo-tions away.

"Let's go home, because we've got unfinished busi-ness," he said, smiling mischievously.

"I don't know what you're talking 'bout, but it's almost lunch time and I'm hungry."

"Then you better swing by Popeye's and eat while you drive. We fucking when we get home," he declared, getting into the passenger seat.

All I could do was laugh as I got in the driver's seat and pointed the car in the direction of the nearest Popeye's. I wasn't about to eat while I was driving and get my steering wheel all greasy. So his ass was gonna have to wait a minute once we got home.

Ten minutes into our drive, my phone rang.

"Answer that baby," I said, pulling into the drive-through.

It was comical watching Big fumble with my phone, trying to use his fingerprint to unlock it, and as expected, by the time he got to where he could answer it, it stopped ringing.

"You laughing now, but you won't be when I throw this bitch out the window," he said sourly.

"You can afford to buy me a new one."

My phone started ringing again, but so did his, so he tossed mine at me and answered his.

"What's up, Joey?" I answered, still laughing.

"I'm sending you a video. Watch it," my lawyer replied, hanging up.

I would've called him back to correct his rudeness, but I could already see Big looking at something on his phone. Once I finally got the video pulled up, I couldn't believe what I was seeing, but one look at Big told me that what I was seeing was real.

"It's only a matter of time now," I said.

Aryanna

Chapter 9
Ebony

"Ms. Dahl? Hi, I'm Jared from customer service. While your plane is being refueled, I was told to escort you and your companion to our V.I.P. waiting lounge."

"Lead the way," I said, stepping away from the ticket counter and following the slim-built white man.

After waiting twenty minutes already to be told whether we could board or not, I guess they'd seen that I was about to go commercial just to get us the fuck away from here. Justice and I were in agreement that it didn't matter what the destination was. We simply needed to put the state of California in the rearview. I hadn't exactly been quiet about my displeasure at having to wait either, which meant this V.I.P. lounge was undoubtedly their lame attempt at pacifying us.

"Where exactly is this lounge?" Justice whispered to me once we'd passed through two sets of double doors.

"J, you know exactly how many times I've been in this airport."

"Yeah, but I thought one was just like the next when it comes to the V.I.P. treatment, and we both know that you'd know about that," he replied, swatting me on the ass.

"I got a little ratchet in me too though," I said, smiling at him over my shoulder.

"Yeah, and I love - "

His abrupt pause in speech and sudden bug-eyed look made me turn my attention back in front of me, and I did so just in time to stop myself from running face first into a gun barrel. Jared from customer service was no longer wearing a plastic smile as he held a Glock .40 inches from my nose, but he was wearing a badge. And he'd brought some friends with him.

"I'm pregnant," I said immediately, putting my hands straight up.

"Then don't resist, turn around, and put your hands behind your back," Jared instructed.

I slowly put my purse on the ground in front of me before doing as I was told.

"Your turn," Jared said, obviously talking to Justice.

I could see the will to resist in his eyes, but we were outmanned, and severely outgunned. Because of how strict airport security was we hadn't even thought to attempt to bring a weapon inside, which meant unless Justice wanted us to become confetti, he had to comply. When our eyes met, I was relieved to see that he understood that, and he slowly turned around and put his hands behind his back. Both of us were swiftly cuffed, and then we were marched to an open door a couple feet way. We were pushed inside, and the door was quickly closed.

"Oh God, this is b- "

"Shhh! The rooms probably wired for sound," Justice said, looking around.

I'd thought that because it was just the two of us in here that we were alone, but his statement made it clear that I was being naïve. I'd just killed three people, one of whom was a cop, and a recorded confession would be enough for the state of California to return the favor by swiftly executing my high yellow ass.

"This shit is *crazy!*" I stated, shaking my head in disbelief.

"I know, but we'll be okay. No matter what happens, you know not to say shit until your lawyer gets here."

"Do you think they'll give us a phone call?" I asked.

"They *have* to give us a call, baby, and if they say something differently, they're lying."

Since he was way more versed in the procedures of due process than I was, I trusted what he was saying. What I had questions about was any lawyer's ability to get me out of this.

"You okay?" Justice asked suddenly.

"N-no, I don't feel good," I said, bending over at the waist.

He immediately moved to my side, but both of us being handcuffed prevented him from wrapping his arms around me to give me the comfort I needed.

"EB, you *gotta* remain calm. You know how bad stress is for the baby, and I know it's impossible not to be stressed right now, but we'll figure this shit out, I promise."

"Uh huh," I replied weakly, taking slow, deep breaths in an attempt to slow down my racing heart. Finding calm in this situation seemed as impossible as rewinding time, but after several minutes, I managed to stand up straight again.

"You don't look like you're ready to puke anymore," he observed.

"If that's your idea of a compliment or some sweet talk, it's not, and you suck at it."

My statement made him chuckle, which actually took away some of the terror I was feeling. Without warning, he leaned in and kissed me on the cheek, and then his lips moved further up to my ear.

"I won't let anything happen to you or our baby. Even if I have to go to jail. I'll protect you both, I promise," he whispered before kissing me again and stepping back to look down at me.

I nodded in understanding, fighting against the tears in my throat while offering him my lips to kiss. The way our mouths joined spoke to equal parts of fear and desperation, but it was understood that there was nothing we could do about it. So we just kissed.

"Isn't that sweet," a voice said, startling us.

Standing in the open doorway was a short, round, white man with salt and pepper hair and a thick mustache that had obviously been dyed an unbelievable dark brown.

"Don't let me interrupt. After all, these could be your last moments together," he said, stepping into the room with two massive black dudes in tow.

"We ain't got shit to say except that we'd like to make a call to a lawyer," Justice stated, stepping protectively in front of me.

Without a word, the white dude pointed a finger at Justice, and his two henchmen moved on him quick. I could feel Justice tense up against the blows that we were both anticipating, but instead, one of the men turned him around while the other uncuffed him.

"You're free to go," the white man said.

"Wh-what?" I asked, feeling disbelief and relief flood my veins, as I wanted to be uncuffed.

"Oh, I'm sorry, Ms. Dahl, I didn't mean to give you the impression that *you* were free to go. You're not. However, the United States Marshal Service has no interest in whatever your new boy toy is, so he's free to go."

"U.S. Marshal Service? Who the fuck are you, and what's this about?" Justice asked, still not moving from in front of me.

Even though he had his hands free now, I still didn't like his odds of not getting fucked up by the two niggas who were now looking at him like he was lunch.

"My name is Arthur, and since my business isn't with you, that's all the information you're getting. Now you can either walk out of here, or my two friends can carry you out," Arthur replied, smiling.

"They don't weigh enough," Justice stated arrogantly.

I couldn't see his face because he had his back to me, but I could tell just by the tone of voice that he was ready to get on his bullshit. I'd expected some type of command to come from Arthur before shit went bad, but that ain't how it went. The nigga standing the closest to us fired a neck-snapping upper cut that instantly had Justice looking at the ceiling, and before he could recover, a right hook had him sliding to the floor beside me.

"Kindly escort him out and have a taxi drop him off," Arthur instructed.

I was still in disbelief, but the fat man in front of me was completely calm. He watched in boredom while I watched in horror as Justice was carried from the room like wet laundry.

"Now that that's taken care of, why don't we get down to business, shall we?"

"What-what do you want from me?" I asked hesitantly.

"For you to play nice so that I can put these on you," he replied, holding up a pair of thick black flex cuffs.

"I won't do any-anything. Just don't hurt my - "

"Your baby, I know, I was told by the cops who detained you that you claimed to be pregnant," he said.

"I *am* pregnant."

"Congratulations. But just so you know juries still find pregnant women guilty. Turn around," he demanded.

Just hearing the words "jury" and "guilty" left me feeling dazed, but I still complied with his demands. Within a matter of moments, cold steel was exchanged for hard plastic, and then I was allowed to turn back around to face my captor.

"Now what?" I asked.

"Well, now we board a plane and we send you to face the music, but don't worry, you're still flying private."

"Flying? I don't understand. Where are you taking me?" I asked, completely confused.

"Texas, where else?"

"Texas? Why the hell would you be arresting me to take me to Texas?" I asked, feeling slight relief to go with my confusion.

"You're really gonna pretend that you don't know that you have a warrant for your arrest in Texas?" he asked, smirking at me.

"A warrant? In Texas? That's seriously why you've got me cuffed? Even if I had a warrant in Texas, it's probably for some dumb shit like driving without a license, which means you must feel real important apprehending such a dangerous criminal," I replied sarcastically.

I wanted to laugh out loud and tell this short, fat, fucker just how stupid he was because he was about to help me escape what I'd just been forced to do. I kept the truth inside though and simply shook my head in disbelief.

"Ebony, I know you didn't graduate college, but from the transcripts I've seen you appeared to be an intelligent young woman. So I ask you, do you think the *United Stated Marshalls* are deployed for the apprehension of someone who has to be in court for any type of traffic violation?"

It wasn't his question or the condescending tone that coated his words that made me pause. It was the look in his eyes. I'd spent enough time around uppity rich types to know what it looked like when people actually believed they were superior to you. It was obvious that this man knew at least the basics about me, which meant that he knew I could buy and sell his ugly ass, yet he still looked at me without fear or respect. To me, that meant he thought that he had me in a corner, and I was getting a bad feeling that he was right.

"Okay, I'll bite. What does the great state of Texas want with little old me?" I asked with false bravado.

"You're going to face the murder that you've been indicted for."

I stood there staring at him waiting on him to give me the reason because there was no *way* he just said I'd been indicted for murder. When he said nothing more, I shook my head hoping to somehow unclog my ears.

"Say that again," I stated.

"Oh, I know you heard me, but I'll say it slowly for you. Mur-der - first degree, to be exact."

"Get the fuck out of here! Do you know who I am? Who my family is? I ain't gotta kill people," I said adamantly.

"Hey, listen, I'm not here to judge you. My only job is to get you back home so that you can face the music," he replied, pulling his phone out of his cargo pants pocket.

Him stepping out of the room to take his call was the only thing that stopped me from screaming at him until he understood that somebody somewhere had made a mistake. A *serious* mistake! Suddenly my mind flashed to Soloman. With everything that had happened, I'd stopped paying attention to what had been going on in Fort Worth, and that oversight was now here to haunt me. I'd been hoping that with Ivy dead all that shit would simply fade away, especially since Justice had convinced me that Big wanted me dead instead of in jail. Apparently me being dead or on death row was the same thing. As badly as I wanted to remain strong in the face of this adversity, I couldn't stop the tears that were now sliding soundlessly down my face. Part of me had sincerely believed that Justice could protect me from what had happened in the restaurant, but how could he protect me from this? I would be viewed as a cold-hearted murder for executing a man incapable of defending himself.

"Sorry, that was my boss. All your questions will be answered once I get you back to Fort Worth, so let's go," Arthur said, waving me towards the door.

I didn't think my legs would carry me, but somehow I was able to put one foot in front of the other and cross the room. His two goons met us right outside the door, but sadly, there was no sign of Justice anywhere. I was grabbed by each of my arms and escorted behind Arthur, who led the way through a side door outside. We crossed to a private hanger and boarded a black G2. No sooner had the stairs been pulled in and the door secured than I heard the engines fired up, and then we were rolling towards a runway. Fifteen minutes later, the sunny state of California was a fleeting speck as we blew through clouds that were dark and ominous.

I spent the entire flight trying to formulate some type of defense in my mind, but everything I came up with sounded like *bullshit*. I was gonna need one hell of a lawyer, maybe even two. The only lawyer I knew was Ivy's, and it seemed stupid to call for any type of help. Just thinking about him made me wonder if he'd put some loophole in the paperwork he'd put together regarding my mom's estate. It wouldn't surprise me to find that Ivy had put me on death row *and* managed to bankrupt me, all from her comfortable spot in the grave. It seemed like the bitch stayed a step ahead no matter what I did!

Once we landed, I was shoved into the back of a waiting Suburban, and a half hour later I was being booked on one count of murder in the first degree. My arraignment was scheduled for tomorrow morning, but I had no illusions that I'd be given any type of bond, especially when the shit that happened in Cali caught up to me. I was stripped of my clothes, along with my dignity, and then I was tossed into a cell. The only good thing I could find to hold onto was the fact that the nurse who'd examined me had been nice, and she promised to look in on me regularly.

I was given a cell by myself, but it damn sure wasn't the Marriot. After taking the time to carefully inspect every inch of the mattress and bunk I was expected to sleep on, I made my bed and crawled into a ball beneath the covers. I just knew that I'd be up half the night listening to all the noises and screams from people I couldn't see, but sheer exhaustion forced sleep upon it. I didn't dream - or at least, I hadn't thought I'd been dreaming until the sound of my door being shaken forced my eyes back open. The constant illumination from the dim hanging light prevented me from telling how much time had passed, but I immediately saw something I didn't believe.

"I wish I could kill you again," I said.

"Wow, sis, is that anyway to greet me?"

"We're not sisters, Ivy. You're a ghost or dream, or whatever the fuck you are, and I'm here stuck in the mess you made," I said, wishing my gun would materialize in my hand.

I actually looked at my palm expecting to find a pistol, there because that's how shit worked in dreams. Hearing that bitch's familiar snicker made me look back at the door again.

"Death is funny, huh?" I asked.

"I'm laughing at the fact that you still think I'm dead."

Chapter 10
Ivy

I could tell with each second that passed that the fog of sleep was slowly clearing from her brain, but this reality wasn't a truth that she'd come to accept yet.

"What makes you think I'm dead, EB?" I asked.

"I *know* that you're dead because I know who killed you. Plus you and your sainted father made the news like you two were pillars of the community, when really both of you were - "

"*Don't* speak about my father, bitch," I warned aggressively.

"But I have so much to say about the now-famous Soloman Black. When I'm done, he'll be infamous, though, because if you think I'm about to go on trial for his murder without airing *all* of his dirty laundry, then you got me fucked up, *sis*."

For a moment her statement confused me, but it didn't take me long to realize that she was actually the one confused.

"It sounds to me like you've made a very wrong assumption, Ebony, so I would watch what you say," I advised.

Her laughter before she pulled the covers back over her head was a clear indication of her disbelief and stubbornness, which meant I had to go with option B.

"Open the door," I said, looking at Chief Stringer standing beside me.

"Ivy, I told you that I can't let you kill her while she's in my custody," he replied adamantly.

"I'm not gonna kill her. But the dumb bitch thinks she's locked up for killing Dad. She even thinks I'm a figment of her imagination," I said.

"Who-who are you talking to?" Ebony asked shakily.

She was no longer huddled under the covers, but instead sitting straight up on the bed with her feet on the floor, and her eyes straining to see around the corner where Chief Stringer was hiding. I wanted to ignore her question and apply pressure to the chief of police to open this door separating us, but it had taken a lot of cohesion to get me this far. I'd actually had to come up with a brilliant idea in order to get Stringer to let me spend a little time with Ebony, but I'd secretly been hoping that he'd let me kill her. The resolution on his face told me that I'd have to wait to taste that part of my revenge.

"If you really believe that this is a dream, then come over here to the bars and see who I'm talking to," I told Ebony.

"What are you doing?" Stringer whispered furiously.

"Relax, it's all a dream," I replied without taking my eyes off of Ebony.

The uncertainty in her hazel eyes hadn't been there moments before, but it still didn't prevent her from standing up and crossing the room to me. There was no more than a foot between us, but I knew she still wouldn't be able to see Chief Stringer in the shadows, despite how hard she was looking.

"Who were you expecting to see: your mom or your dad?" I asked, smiling.

Anger made her face change colors as she forgot all about the notion of me being a dream, and she shot her arms through the bars with the intention of grabbing me. I saw her move coming, though, which was why I grabbed her hands and leaned back. The result was that her body weight combined with mine made her run head first into the steel bars that made up her cell door, causing a nice crunching sound.

"I bet that hurt, didn't it?" I taunted, managing to break two fingers on her right hand before Stringer could separate us.

"Goddamn, Ivy!" he whispered angrily, pushing me backwards.

The sound of Ebony howling in pain was worth his anger.

"I bet you don't think this is a dream now, do you, *sis*?" I asked, smiling sweetly.

The blood running from the gash in her forehead or her crooked fingers should've been her primary focus, but instead, her eyes were locked on mine. And they were glowing with fear.

"You-you can't be, you can't be alive," she said slowly.

"Well, if your bleeding head and broken fingers don't tell you otherwise, how about a little information? You're currently under arrest for killing Esteban's nephew, not my father. I can't prove that you killed my dad, even though I know your coward ass did it, and you ran away while your husband lay there dying. I can prove that you murdered Rouis Vasqular in a field because you're on video, plus the cops have the gun you used, and they have Rouis's body. That sounds like murder one," I stated.

"I-I-I-"

"I know, you want a lawyer, right? I'm sure that the judge will appoint you one in the morning, but it won't matter though. You're gonna die, Ebony, and so is that baby you're carrying," I vowed, smiling.

The mention of her child immediately changed the fear to terror in her eyes, and I couldn't deny how good that made me feel.

"Make sure that she's taken care of," I said to Chief Stringer before heading for the door.

"I-Ivy, wait. Ivy, please! Not my baby, Ivy! Ivy!" Ebony yelled.

I could still hear her pleading at the top of her lungs as I slipped out of the jail through the same side entrance that I'd been granted access. I quickly slid into the back of the waiting Range Rover, and moments later I was gone as if I'd never been there. I was still smiling when I climbed from the back of the SUV twenty minutes later, but the look on Big's face in the moonlight made me neutralize my facial features.

"Is there a reason that you're standing outside with no shirt on and a gun in your hand?" I asked.

"Don't play with me, Ivy, just get your ass in the house," he replied aggressively.

Ordinarily I wouldn't have let him talk to me like that, but I could tell by the way that his eyes were evaluating his homie's that he was homicide mad.

"It's no one's fault that I was out, so come inside with me so I can explain," I said, taking his hand and undoubtedly saving somebody's life.

I didn't pause in the living room, preferring instead to take our conversation upstairs where we could be alone.

"Where the fuck were you?" he asked hostilely, no sooner had we come into the bedroom.

"I'm gonna give you a few minutes to stop being mad first because I don't like how you're talking to me."

"Ivy," he said, making his warning clear.

"I went to see Ebony," I replied, letting his hand go and turning away from him while getting undressed.

He didn't say anything, but then again, he didn't really have to. After we'd both watched the surveillance video earlier of her being apprehended at the airport he'd known that I wanted to be face to face with that bitch, and he'd said no before I could suggest it. Since I hadn't asked, though, I hadn't technically disobeyed him or his wishes. Somehow I knew that technicality wouldn't win any arguments though. I turned back around to find him standing in the same spot, but there was a new level of pissed contorting his features.

"Before you yell at me or shoot me, I want you to listen to the idea that I had," I said, walking over to him and standing in front of him.

I knew how beautiful I looked naked in the moonlight streaming through the windows, but he didn't even glance at what I had to offer. That meant he was madder then I'd thought.

"A'ight, here's the play. We know that they have enough for a conviction, which either means life in prison or that nice cocktail that she never wakes up from. Both of those are good options, but I thought of another one. What if she was found to be mentally incapable to stand trial?"

"Then she'd spend some time in a puzzle factory, and be released," he replied.

"Right, and then I could really make her pay for what she's done," I said, smiling.

"How is she gonna make them believe that she's crazy though?"

"What else are they gonna think when she keeps crying out for a dead person?" I asked, grinning devilishly.

For a second he starred at me, and then he chuckled while shaking his head.

"Tell me what you did," he said.

I quickly ran down my visit with my former best friend, enjoying being able to relive smashing her face into the bars and breaking her fingers.

"Sounds like you had fun, but that don't excuse the sneaky shit you did, Ivy."

"If I had told you what I had in mind and asked your permission to go, would you have agreed?" I asked.

"No."

"Exactly, because to you, nothing is more important than keeping the fact that I'm alive a secret, and I understand that. I hope that you can understand why it needs to be me that kills her," I said.

"I get it, but just because you can make her see dead people don't mean you're plan is gonna work. So was it really worth the risk?" he asked.

"I only told you the first part of the plan, babe. Right now, as we speak, Ebony is meeting with the jail psychologist, who is of course bought and paid for, and by the time her preliminary trial date comes around, the foundation for an insanity plea will be laid. Ebony would be stupid to ask for an independent doctor, but if she does, we'll be sure to buy them too."

"And what if they can't be bought?" he asked logically.

I took the Ruger 9mm from his hand and held it up so the moonlight could slow dance with the chrome and wood. With my other hand, I grabbed his dick through his shorts.

"You see, baby, what makes us such an effective team is that we're each other's counterparts. Guerilla tactics are your bread and butter, while rubbing elbows is mine, but both approaches are needed to conquer the world and everything in it. I understand the power of money just as well as you understand the power of this pistol in my hand - and the dick too, for that matter. So is it really a questions of whether or not we'll accomplish what we must?" I asked.

"No, it's not. Don't think that means you can be sneaky or deceptive when you want to, though, because that ain't how we get down."

"Understood. How can I make it up to you, baby?" I asked seductively.

He took the gun from my hand and tossed it on the bed before pushing his shorts to the floor.

"You know what I like," he replied.

"Indeed I do."

It only took seconds to get him harder than the bars I'd pulled Ebony into, but when I went to get on my knees, he stopped me.

"I thought that this was what you wanted," I said.

"I do, but I wanna take it back in the day one time. Up against the wall."

"You mean - "

"You know *exactly* what I mean," he said, grinning hard.

Even though it seemed inappropriate, I had to laugh because we hadn't done what he suggested in a long time, but it was always fun.

"You sure that you're up for all that?" I asked seriously.

"Are you?"

"Well, there's only one way to find out," I replied, stepping away from him and going to the nearest wall.

After taking the appropriate stance, I looked at him.

"You do remember my safe word, right?" I asked.

His laughter worried me a little, but I let it slide because I knew that he knew better than to hurt me, or let me hurt myself. I took a deep breath before executing a perfect handstand up against the wall. I was amazed to have gotten it on the first try, and the applause that Big gave me showed that he was too.

"Eat me," I demanded, spreading my legs.

Without hesitation he grabbed my ankles and lifted me up against the wall until he was eye level with my pussy, and then he feasted. I could tell that he wasn't playing no games because he started off by sucking my clit so hard that I forgot what I was supposed to be doing. Despite my current position, I wasn't just hanging out. Still, it was an effort to concentrate enough for me to wrap my hand around the back of his legs, and pull my upper body towards him. I figured it out quick though, and within moments, I was sucking his dick with equal enthusiasm. The sensations shooting through my body were indescribable. The blood rushing to my head came with bells warning that I could black-out if I wasn't careful, but the alarm sounding off on my first climax drowned out all other noise. I kept up my rhythmic bobbing and technique of trying to suck the skin off the dick, but when that hurricane orgasm made landfall, I had to pause as I fought to hang on to consciousness. I rode the fierce lullaby until the aftershocks set in, and then I got back to work. Under the determined expertise of Big's tongue, I knew I only had a few minutes of sanity left, but I was gonna make them count. I was eating the dick like my momma named me deep throat, and I could feel the trembling in his legs. Not even the sudden spots in my vision could slow me down because I felt him trying to force my surrender with his tongue. He was swimming in the current through my pussy lips to my clit before backstroking to my asshole to dry off. We both knew that him sticking his tongue in my ass wasn't fair, but I didn't care because every time his dick punched the back of my throat, I felt the shaking in his body become more pronounced.

When I felt his grip on my ankles tighten to the point that it hurt, I knew I had him. A few seconds later, his cum shot into my mouth with enough force to send some down my throat and up into my nasal passage at the same time, causing me to choke. When I released his dick from my mouth, I had time to take one deep breath before that hurricane made landfall again and took me underwater. I knew that I had to be a sight to see with cum leaking from my mouth, nose, *and* pussy as I hung upside down, but at the moment, I didn't give a fuck.

"U-umbrella," I finally choked out.

In an instant, he had me flipped around and he was cradling me in his arms, taking me to the bed.

"Did you forget that you can't swallow when you're upside down?" he asked, clearly fighting not to laugh.

"F-fuck you."

Now he did laugh, but at least he wiped the cum off of my face while he did it.

"You owe me," I stated.

"Do I? Well, you know I always pay my debts."

"Baby-baby, wait," I said once he laid me down.

Of course he didn't, though, and a few moments later, I was begging him not to stop.

Aryanna

Chapter 11
Ebony
Two days later

"It doesn't matter how many different ways that you ask me the same question because you're gonna get the same answer. Ivy Black is *alive*, and I saw her with my own two eyes!" I stated slowly.

"Okay, how about we try a different approach. You say that Ivy is alive, and from all the information that I gathered in the past couple days, you and her grew up closer than sisters. So why would she cause that wound to your head, and break your fingers? Why would she threaten to kill you and your unborn child?" Dr. Phillips asked.

Despite my growing anger and unstable emotional state, I knew better than to blurt out the truthful answer to that question. I had no doubt that this blonde-haired bitch sitting across from me thought that I was crazy, but I knew the truth. Ivy had given me a concussion and broken my index and middle fingers on my left hand, but she'd also told me some true shit. I wasn't locked up for killing her dad, which meant that I couldn't tell this mental health doctor they'd sent to evaluate me why Ivy really wanted me and my baby dead. Fighting one murder charge was hard enough.

"Ivy and I had a falling out over a man," I replied shortly.

"And that's enough to make her want to kill you and your innocent little baby."

"Yes! She's crazy!" I said emphatically.

"You mentioned losing your first child not long ago, as well as your parents. Have you grieved for them? And if so, how?"

Given our current topic of conversation these were the last questions I'd expected her to ask, and I really didn't want to answer them because I knew she had an agenda for asking them.

"I don't want to talk about that," I replied.

"Why not? Grief is a natural thing when we lose those that we love, and death is a part of life."

"Please don't come at me with the bumper sticker bull-shit, and just drop it. I said I don't wanna talk about it," I reiterated aggressively.

"I think that you *need* to talk about it," she insisted gently.

What I really needed was to escape from this little-ass room before I beat this bitch up in here! Even though we were sitting across from each other in comfortable chairs with plush carpet under our feet, there were still cameras around, and that was saving her. I kept my mouth shut for a full count of ten in hopes of suppressing my anger and that she would see the wisdom in moving on to the next topic of conversation. I should've known better though because people in her career field were skilled at the art of enduring, and manipulating, silences.

"Why are you asking me about my grief and grieving process?" I asked.

"Because it's important to know that you went through those things given all that you've lost."

"Yeah, well, there's no handbook on how to grieve. All you can do is take it day by day and pray that you don't drown in the fast-moving water that is grief," I said truthfully.

"Sounds like you've had to do some navigation your-self in order for you to understand it."

I nodded my head slowly, hoping that this woman re-ally wasn't about to make me go back down the rabbit hole to relive the worst tines of my life.

"Let me ask you this. Was Ivy there for you while you grieved?" she asked.

"No."

"Not at all? I mean, you two were best friends, so why wouldn't she be there in your time of need?" Dr. Phillips asked.

"I told you, we had a falling out."

"Well, I can imagine how angry that must've made you that you two couldn't put your differences aside. I'm sure that whatever disagreement you had wasn't more important than what was going on in your life," she said sympatheti-cally.

"I didn't want her pity or support," I said honestly.

I wouldn't tell the sweet doctor what I'd *truly* wanted. For a while, I'd thought that I had what I'd wanted, but apparently this bitch Ivy was harder to get rid of than a yeast infection. She had to die though, before she had a chance to make good on her promise.

"Dr. Phillips, I know that you think I'm crazy, but I'm not. I have no reason to make up the fact that Ivy's still alive."

"Unless you're finally admitting that you miss her, and you're scared because you're about to be a single mother," Dr. Phillips said.

"I'm sorry, what did you say?"

"You heard me, Ebony," she replied patiently.

I wanted to head butt this bitch in the nose, but I somehow managed to resist the urge. Just barely. I had to admit that she was a bold mu'fucka though.

"How about we drop the subject of Ivy for this session, because it's really starting to upset me and the baby," I suggested.

"I'm not trying to upset you. I'm simply trying to understand chaos you have to be going through in order to truly believe that your best friend is alive. It hasn't been very long since she passed, so maybe your brain is still trying to process the loss."

"Whatever you say, Doc, but right now, I don't wanna talk about it," I replied stubbornly.

"I understand. We can pick up where we left off in our next session.

I wanted to tell her to leave and never come back, but thanks to Ivy's sneaky ass, I now had court mandated psychologist appointments until my preliminary court appearance. So I couldn't avoid the good doctor, but I could damn sure afford a good lawyer to help expedite this whole process along. I wasn't safe in here. Hell I wasn't safe anywhere with Ivy out there lurking, but here in her backyard was the worst place to be. Now that I was on the psych's radar they could find me hanging in my cell, and they probably wouldn't ever suspect foul play! I couldn't go out like that, which meant that I couldn't let this bitch box me in.

"I appreciate you coming to see me," I said, extending my hand to her.

We shook firmly, and then I stood up to leave. The officer saw me through the window and had the door buzzed open so that he could handcuff me. He made sure to give me a thorough pat down first.

"Next time, buy me dinner first," I said sarcastically.

"I'll do more than that if you're nice," he whispered, pulling my handcuffed wrists roughly.

I had another smart reply on the tip of my tongue, but I thought better of it as he pushed me down the hallway. When I went to turn down the hallway that led back to my cell, he snatched me by my cuffs and steered me down the opposite hall.

"Where are you taking me?" I asked.

"Why, you scared?" he retorted.

The truth was that I kinda was, but I damn sure wasn't about to say that to this mu'fucka.

"Scared? No. Hungry and ready for a nap is what I am."

"Well, I can always tell your lawyer that you refused your visit, he said, halting our forward progress so that he could look at me

"I'd never be dumb enough to refuse an attorney visit."

"Right, you're just dumb enough to kill a guy on tape," he replied, chuckling as we started down the hall again.

If my hands weren't cuffed, I would've turned his pale white face several different shades of red, but instead, I turned my attention and focus on my visit. Technically I hadn't hired a lawyer yet, but I guess the courts were obligated to give me one. I remembered hearing something about it at my arraignment, but honestly, it had been hard to pay attention because the moment was too surreal. I never imagined that I'd ever end up in this situation, and I'd lost track of how many times I'd convinced myself that this was someone else's life. I wasn't about to tell Dr. Phillips that though, and I doubted my lawyer would care. I was just hoping whoever he or she was could tell me exactly what I was looking at.

This visit in general had been a surprise, but when the officer showed me into the room at the end of the hall, my jaw hit the floor. I didn't say anything until the cuffs were off and the door behind us was closed.

"Ms. Dahl, I'm Stephanie Yanis, and I'm your lawyer. I'm sure that you know who this is," she said, gesturing towards the man in the charcoal suit sitting next to her.

"Are there cameras in here?" I asked.

"Video, but no audio," she replied.

Mentally I allowed this information to sink in because every bone in my body was screaming for me to hurl myself into Justice's arms.

"Can I just tell you that you're the best thing I've ever seen, and it's not because you clean up real nice with a suit on," I said, smiling with relief as I sat across from them.

"Right back at you, sweetheart. How are you holding up?" he asked, unable to hide the concern on his face.

"I'm fine, J, don't worry."

"Good. Then explain to me what the *fuck* happened to you," he said, allowing his anger to rush to the surface.

"That's an interesting story for later, but I promise you that me and the baby are fine for now," I replied.

"For now? What does that mean, Ebony? Is someone in here threatening you and my baby?" he asked.

"Not exactly. All I mean is that I need to get the fuck out of here because this is the last place I need to be."

"On that we all agree, Ms. Dahl, but I need to be completely honest with you about how ugly this situation is right now," Stephanie said.

"Don't sell me a dream. Tell me exactly how ugly it is," I replied, mentally bracing myself.

"Okay, well, normally I'd have to wait until closer to the preliminary to find out everything the prosecution has, but they were only too happy to give it to me. I've seen the tape, and it's certainly damaging."

"What happened, EB?" Justice asked.

"The dude I shot was the one who killed my mom. You remember that night."

"The recording doesn't start until you're standing over him with the gun in your hand, and the angle it was shot from only shows your face clearly. I'm gonna assume that you didn't know that you were being recorded," Stephanie said.

"No, it didn't even cross my mind that Ivy would pull a move like that. Honestly, I was completely focused on the mu'fucka who'd taken my mom from me."

"Conniving bitch," Justice growled, shaking his head.

"Believe it or not, your warring emotions are clear to intercept on the recording, and right before it ended it shows you stepping into a young woman's open arms. If we take this to trial I'll definitely argue that it was a crime of passion," Stephanie stated.

"You said *if* we take it to trial. What are my other options?" I asked.

Even though I'd pleaded not guilty at arraignment, I wasn't dumb enough to think I stood any more than a slight chance if I went into a court and denied everything. The jury wouldn't even have to leave the room to deliberate.

"Well, you can take a plea now, but they're only offering twenty-five years to be served at eight-five percent," she replied hesitantly.

"Twenty-five -twenty-five years," I said, barely able to get the words out of my mouth.

"Not happening," Justice stated decidedly.

"That means that we could go with the defense of it not being you, but with all the evidence the state has against you, it's gonna be laughable, and the courts will likely sentence you harshly out of spite because you're not remorse-ful. So in my mind, that leaves out best defense as a plea of not guilty by reason of temporary insanity," she concluded.

I looked from her to Justice and then back to her. And then burst out laughing.

"EB, I know how it sounds, but I don't think there's any other way out of this," Justice said gently.

I heard his words, but I could only laugh harder. Through the tears in my eyes, I could see them exchange a look of worry, which forced me to try and get myself to-gether before I was fitted for a straitjacket right now.

"Are you-are you okay?" Stephanie asked hesitantly.

"I-I'm good, I'm sorry. It's just ironic because right be-fore this visit I was having a session with the psychologist."

"For what?" Justice asked quickly.

"Because they didn't believe me when I told them how I got this knot on my hand and two broken fingers."

"I think now would be a good time to hear that interest-ing story," Stephanie insisted.

I knew Justice would believe me, but I highly doubted that Stephanie would. For that reason, I was hesitant to speak in front of her.

"Trust me, you wouldn't believe me," I replied.

"Try us," Justice said.

I hesitated for a few moments before saying fuck it.

"I was asleep last night and when I woke up, Ivy was at my door. I thought I was dreaming, and I said that to her amongst a few other choice words. She convinced me to come to the door since it was all a dream, and then she said some shit that would've got her ass kicked whether I was dreaming or not. This was the result," I said, holding up my hand and pointing at my face.

As I expected, Stephanie's eyes slid in Justice's direction, but his eyes remained fixed on me.

"She's alive?" he asked.

"As sure as I'm sitting here in front of you."

"But how-."

"Stephanie can you give us a minute?" Justice asked, cutting off her question.

I thought that she might try to ask me again, but instead she got up and quietly left the room.

"Ebony, you know that I love you, but I gotta ask...Are you sure?"

"Yes, she's alive, Justice, and she vowed that me and our baby would die."

The moment those words escaped from in between my lips I wanted them back because I knew Justice would throw caution to the wind, and gun straight for Ivy now. The look of darkness that took over his face only confirmed my suspicions.

"Justice, you need to think for a minute before you make any rash decisions, because you best believe that Big has got her more protected than the president."

"Presidents get assassinated," he replied shortly.

"I understand that, but think about it. For two weeks she's somehow convinced the world that she no longer exists, which means she's up to something. Until we have at least a hint as to what's going on you can't try any dumb shit. Besides, we have enough to worry about."

"If you're talking about what happened in Oakland, that's taken care of. We're good," he replied.

I had a lot of questions about how that was possible, but I trusted him so I stayed focused on the problem at hand.

"My point for telling you and Stephanie about Ivy is because now they think I'm seeing shit, I'm crazy, and I'm grieving. So all I gotta do is keep telling the truth because they don't believe me any fucking way."

"Okay. But what happens if Ivy comes at you again?" he asked logically.

"Let's hope she doesn't, but if she does, I'ma do my best to kill her. What's one more murder between friends?"

Chapter 12
Ivy
Three days later

"Juanito, it's good to see you," I said, gesturing for him to take a seat in the chair across the desk from me.

"Likewise. You look better than when I last saw you, which means that you're recovering nicely."

"I'm trying. As much as I want to move around and be more hands on, Big isn't hearing it," I replied.

"Where is Big anyway?"

"Out in the trenches. He likes to hover over me, so every so often I have to push him out of the house to keep his mind centered on what's going on," I replied.

"Ah. He told me that you've made progress with Ebony and that she is now in police custody out here. What's your next play?" he asked.

"Well, I want to simply kill her and be done with it, but an opportunity presented itself that's too good to pass up. I found out that Ebony is pregnant right now, and I have no doubt that Justice thinks he's the father. Even if he's not biologically, he'd still want to consider that his kid because of his loyalty to Ebony, and because of the fact that he lost his son."

"So you're thinking that Ebony being in danger will flush him out?" Juanito asked thoughtfully.

"Oh, I know it will, which is why I want Big's people to come back down here, but I didn't wanna make that move and leave your men vulnerable without talking to you."

"I like the way that you think, and the consideration that you show. You're a remarkable woman," he said.

I was surprised, and a little embarrassed, to feel myself blushing, especially because I didn't know if it was from his compliment or the way he was smiling at me. Even as a married woman, I had to acknowledge that Juanito was a whole different level of sexy. To be more accurate, he was a pretty gangster. Standing six foot, weighing about two hundred forty pounds, he had those chiseled features that made bitches swoon on the soap operas on Telemundo. There was no doubt that if he took his hair out of its neatly kept ponytail and spoke in his native tongue while staring at you deeply with his dark brown eyes that he'd be trouble. Trouble was the last think that I needed in my life at the moment.

"Thank you, Juanito, your compliment means a lot. I simply try to do things the way that my father would've done them," I stated honestly.

"I never had the privilege of working with your father, but I've long heard of the type of man that he was. You have the same type of character, and that's rare in this business. It'll take you far though."

His statement, while again complimentary, was a reminder that I was now entrenched in this way of life forever. Becoming a mother didn't somehow give me the option to say that I didn't wanna play this game anymore because the reality was that we were not playing. This shit was real, and it was all or nothing.

"How much time do you need to prepare your people in Cali?" I asked.

"That depends. Do you think Justice is back in Texas already?"

"I'd say that's a safe bet, but I haven't decided on a course of action to lure him out yet," I replied.

"You should consider that he might play offense instead of defense, which means that he could move against Big out here."

"That move makes sense, but he'd still be expecting Big to have his people in Cali. If he makes that move, it'll be a miscalculation that leads to his ending," I said.

"In that case, I'll make the necessary calls immediately so that your people can be here sometime tonight. I'll have some of my people come back too," he offered.

"You sure that's not gonna put you in a bad spot?"

"Trust me, manpower isn't something that we lack. Besides, protecting our investment is important enough to have all hands on deck," he replied.

"I appreciate that. Why don't I call Big real quick while you call your people?" I suggested.

He nodded his head in agreement while pulling the phone from his pocket and excusing himself. I picked up the phone off my desk and called Big. When my call went to voicemail after two rings I was surprised, but when that happened twice in a row, something like worry touched me. I waited a couple minutes before calling back, and this time the phone was answered on the first ring. It wasn't my man's voice though.

"Who is this?" I asked immediately.

"This is Star, who is this?" she asked with attitude.

"This is Big's wife. Why are you answering my nigga's phone?"

"Oh, because he's in the middle of something. I'll tell him to call you though," she replied, hanging up.

My anger came in an instant, wrapping me up in its warmth while whispering in my ear the things I should do to this bitch answering my husband's phone. I knew I was trippin' by thinking the thoughts that I was thinking because I trusted Big unequivocally. There was a logical explanation, and I would wait to hear it before I snapped out like some jealous bitch who was insecure. It was a struggle to maintain my composure, but I did it and simply sent Big a text telling him to call me whenever he got a second. After that, I tried to put what had just happened out of my mind, which took a lot of effort.

"Everything is good on my end, how about you?" Juanito asked, coming back into the room and sitting down.

"Big is in a meeting, but he'll call me as soon as he finishes up and I'll let him know what's going on."

"Okay. Before I came here today, I sat down with Manuel because we both wanted to give you a gift to show our appreciation and respect," he said.

Before I could tell him that they didn't have to do that, or ask what my present was, he pulled a pistol from behind his back and stood up.

"It's-it's beautiful," I said, accepting it from him.

It was a Smith and Wesson .45, solid gold with black ivory in place of the wood in the handle. I could tell that it was custom made, one of a kind, because my name was spelled out in gold vines on both sides of the handle. I popped the clip out to find it fully loaded with hollow point slugs.

"It's clean and untraceable," he stated.

"I love it, Juanito, thank you."

"You're welcome. We hope that it comes in handy when you need it the most, and if - "

"Ms., Black, there's a situation at the front gate," James said from my office doorway.

"What kind of situation?" I asked, sliding the clip back into my gun and pulling the slide.

"There's a Mr. Louis Jones out front demanding to see Big, but he's not on the list. What do you want me to do?"

Louis was definitely a friend and business partner, so I didn't feel like I had anything to fear. The only problem was that he didn't know that I was alive. It had to be an emergency for him to show up at the house unannounced, which meant that I couldn't ignore him because that was me ignoring my business and responsibilities.

"Show him in," I replied.

"Is everything okay?" Juanito asked once James disappeared.

"I don't know."

I truly had no idea why Louis was here, or why the fuck Big wasn't answering his damn calls, because I had no doubt that Louis would've called before showing up.

"If you need privacy, I can leave and - "

"No, I don't want you to leave until I know exactly what's going on, but I would appreciate it if you could wait in the living room," I said.

"No problem."

He flashed a smile at me that made me grip the pistol in my hand tighter to steady myself and focus on business, instead of whatever wild thoughts that wanted to race through my mind. Big and I were both of the belief that it was okay to admire the opposite sex, but not in a lustful way. For reasons that I couldn't explain, Juanito was testing the limitations in my mind of what was appropriate.

Thankfully Louis entered my study, and his disheveled appearance made it obvious where my attention was needed.

"You've certainly see better days," I said.

"I-Ivy? Oh my God, Ivy!" Louis said, swiftly moving towards me and hugging me tightly.

"Easy, love, I'm alive, but I was still shot."

"I'm sorry, I just - Wow, you're alive! How-when-how?" he replied, clearly at a loss for words.

I could hear that Juanito was chuckling as he and James quietly left, but I was focused on the man in front of me and not the comedy.

"Sit down and tell me what's going on," I said.

My request immediately transformed his expression from surprised delight to utter sadness.

"I'm glad you're alive. It makes me feel safer than I did a few minutes ago."

"What happened?" I asked patiently.

"It's-it's Jeremy. Him and his family were murdered."

"What? When?" I asked rapidly.

"Just-just a few hours ago is when they were found. It was *horrific*, Ivy."

"Tell me everything that you know," I demanded.

"I got a call from my brother asking me if I'd talked to Jeremy because we were supposed to get together and go over some numbers. I told him that I hadn't, and he said he was gonna swing by his house. An hour later he called and told me that there were cops everywhere, and that-that there were body parts everywhere too."

I was processing the information as fast as he was giving it to me, but what he'd said took a few extra seconds to compute.

"Body parts? Whose body parts?" I asked slowly.

"Jeremy's, K-Kristen's, and little Harley's too. I vomited as soon as my brother told me that," he confessed.

I could tell by the somewhat far off look in his blue eyes that throwing up might not be far away for him again, and I didn't need that right now.

"What do the cops know?"

"Nothing, I don't think, except for the obvious, which is that they were tortured," he replied.

For someone like Jeremy to be tortured was unusual because he was more or less a white collar criminal, in the respect that he was far removed from the street shit. His only brush with that side of our business came when Justice had tried to take over, and I wasn't naïve enough to believe that this was all a coincidence. If I was right, though, then it was clear that Justice was after information more so than my empire. And I had a hunch as to what he wanted so desperately to know.

"Where's your brother and his family right now?" I asked.

"At home with my wife and kids, waiting on me to bring the cavalry."

"I think it'll be better if they all came here because as you can see, we've made some necessary safety additions.

"You-you would open your house to our family?" he asked, clearly shocked.

"Of course I would, Louis. *We're* family. I want every-body out here as soon as possible."

"I don't know what to say, Ivy."

"There's nothing that needs saying, I'm just sorry that I didn't do something before Jeremy and his family lost their lives," I replied sincerely.

"I know, but this-this life was thrust upon you and shit has come at you from every direction. For Christ's sake, you almost *died*! Still, you rise to the occasion every time, and I thank you for that."

What he said embarrassed me almost as much as what Juanito had said earlier, but I knew he was being genuine. Just like I knew his appreciation was directly related to my dad and the pride he would have in my ability to bounce back. He didn't raise no bitch, He raised *that bitch*.

"James!" I called out.

Moments later, he appeared in the doorway.

"I want you to take some men with you to pick up Louis and his brother Roger's families and bring them back here. And send Juanito back in on your way out."

"Yes, Ms. Black."

"Thank you, Ivy," Louis said again before leaving with James.

I was still trying to organize my thoughts when Juanito came into the study and reclaimed his seat.

"Well, how bad is it?" he asked.

"One of my business partners and his family were killed a little while ago."

"I'm sure that it's safe to assume that this didn't happen by natural causes," he said.

"Far from it. They were chopped up, which signals torture, and my money is on Justice," I stated confidently.

"Why would he go after your business again when he has his hands full trying to stay alive?"

"My best guess is that he was seeking information that was valuable enough to risk taking his eyes off the flying bullets for a moment, and I'm betting that info pertained to me. No doubt his logical conclusion would be that if I was actually alive, I would have my hands in my business," I replied.

"I see. That means your belief about him making contact with Ebony is true, and he's made his first offensive move."

"Seems like we were both right," I said.

"So now what?"

Now was the exact moment where Big's thoughts and opinions were needed, but this mu'fucka was too busy with whatever else. I'd resisted the urge to pick up my phone and check it up until this point, but now I did grab it off the desk and look at the screen. I found what I expected, which was nothing, and that only succeeded in adding to my frustration.

"What do you think I should do?" I asked suddenly.

"Wait."

"Wait," I repeated slowly.

"Yes. Your actions can't simply be a reaction to what he's done because then he's the puppet master pulling your strings. So you wait and strategize your next move, guaranteeing that you're at least one move ahead of your opponent," he replied.

I let his words roll around in my mind like a pinball until all signals pointed towards that being the most logical course of action.

"Wait," I said again.

"Exactly."

"I feel like you're right, but I'm not the most patient person in the world," I admitted.

"You simply need something to distract you," he replied smiling.

Despite his casual delivery, the words he'd spoken sounded entirely too sexual for my liking, but his expression was open and honest.

"I guess I could find something around here to take my mind off of the drama for a little while."

"Actually, I have an idea," he said.

I was damn near afraid to ask, but I knew that was just my overactive imagination reading too deep into nothing.

"What's your idea?" I asked.

"Dinner."

"Dinner? You mean like us go out somewhere?" I asked cautiously.

"No, I know that you're not getting out much these days, but I'm sure that means your kitchen is stocked. I'll cook."

"You cook?" I asked slowly, unable to hide my surprise.

"Of course! My mama would be ashamed of me if I only knew how to kill to survive, but not nourish myself," he replied, laughing.

I laughed too while shaking my head in amazement.

"So you wanna cook for me?"

"If that's okay with you," he replied.

"I'm not gonna believe it until I see it," I said, standing up and tucking my pistol into the waist of my shorts.

I led him to the kitchen, where he told me to have several seats as he got to work. I couldn't pronounce what he was putting together no matter how slowly he said it to me, but it smelled amazing and reminded me of my mother's cooking. When he let me try some, my eyes rolled involuntarily, but I didn't care because it tasted as good as it smelled. The problem was that when I opened my eyes, Big was suddenly standing there, and the look on his face was murderous.

Chapter 13
Ebony

"Wipe your pretty little ass, Dahl, you've got somewhere to be," the officer said from right outside my cell door.

I could feel the skin on my face heating up at the indecency of being caught squatting over the cold steel toilet, but the anger I felt overrode my embarrassment. This officer, Lewellyn, took a sick pleasure in fucking with me in any way that he could, despite my repeated attempts to stay out of his way. Standing there watching me wipe my pussy was the last straw though.

"You really don't know who you're fucking with, but you're gonna learn," I said, pulling my pants up while standing up straight.

"Are you threatening me, inmate Dahl?" he asked sweetly.

I ignored the bait he'd laid out and washed my hands after flushing the toilet. When I backed up to the bars of my cell door, I prepared myself for him to put the handcuffs on extra tight, and I wasn't disappointed. I showed no outward signs of my discomfort though because I knew his nothing ass would be handled.

I was pulled out of my cell and pushed down the hall roughly. But not even that could take the smile off my face because I knew where I was going, and who was waiting on me. A few minutes later, I was led into the attorney visitation room. When I made a move to step further into the room, Officer Lewellyn snatched me backwards by my cuffs, causing me to wince in pain.

"You need to watch how you handle her," Justice said. His tone was calm, but his eyes were blazing with fury.

"Tell your client not to move until instructed."

No one said anything until the cuffs were off me and the officer was gone.

"What's his deal?" Stephanie asked.

"Fuck that, what's his name?" Justice asked aggressively.

"Lewellyn, and his deal is that he likes to fuck with me to pass time. He just watched me wipe myself before bringing me down here," I replied, looking directly at Justice.

"I'll contact the chief of police and - "

"Don't worry about it," Justice said, putting a hand on Stephanie's arm to stop her from writing.

She gave him a brief glance, but he never took his eyes off me.

"O-kay," she said slowly.

"Tell me that you've come with good news," I said, switching our focus to why they were here.

"I wish I had good news, but so far I've found nothing to confirm what you told us. I mean I found *nothing*. Ivy's death certificate is official and properly filed, and all of her assets have been transferred into her husband's name," Stephanie replied.

"She's alive," I stated.

"No one has seen her, there's no record of her leaving the country, and the people I spoke to swear that Ivy's dead," Justice said.

"She's *alive*," I repeated adamantly.

"You know her better than either of us, so where would she run and hide?" Stephanie asked.

"I've been wondering the same thing the last few days, but there's really no way to tell without knowing what the bitch is up to," I replied.

"Ok, well, why would she fake her death anyway?" Stephanie asked.

I looked at Justice, unsure of exactly what he'd told my lawyer, but more than comfortable letting him answer.

"Ivy had a lot of enemies, some that she created, and others that she'd inherited from her father. If she did somehow survive being shot, I'm sure that she would feel safer with the world thinking that she was dead, especially since no one knows who shot her or her father," he replied.

"It's an unsolved murder, just like my father's," I stated evenly.

"I see your point, but none of that explains the official documentation or the cops' consistent story about her being dead," Stephanie said.

"It wouldn't be the first time that money has bought silence," I replied.

The skepticism that Stephanie was trying hard to conceal on her face was starting to piss me off, but I bit my tongue because I understood how wild my accusations were. If I didn't have the physical reminder of my altercation with her, I might not believe my damn self.

"I'll keep looking," Justice vowed.

"Be careful," I warned.

"Okay, so given the fact that you've never been in trouble, I've filed a motion to get you a bond, but given everything that we know *they* know, it's a long shot. You're worth a lot of money though, and that buys you more leverage and leeway than the average criminal. Plus, the fact that you're pregnant gets you sympathy points," Stephanie said.

"When is the hearing?" I asked.

"In the morning. The courts may agree to house arrest, and of course you'd have to forfeit your passport along with your plane," Stephanie replied.

"None of that matters. Just get me out of here," I said.

"Don't worry, you're coming home one way or another," Justice vowed.

The look of unwavering determination on his face actually made me smile.

"I can't wait. I don't know how you spent so much time in places like this, but the boredom alone will drive you fucking crazy!" I said, shaking my head.

"It's easier when you're in general population because you get to move around and do things," he replied.

"Stephanie, can you get me moved to - "

"No, she can't and won't. For one, you're not going near general population while you're pregnant. And two, if Ivy really is alive, you think that she won't have you stabbed to death?" he asked.

"You don't think that she could do all that with me being stuck in a cell?" I countered, holding up my hand, which still sported two splints on my broken fingers.

"It's a moot point because with your wealth and connections, they wouldn't trust anyone not to be tempted to let you out of a side door," Stephanie said.

I wouldn't insult her intelligence by telling her that I would never indulge in that type of shit. I'd done worse, and I would do worse for my freedom.

"Don't you need to make that call?" Justice asked Stephanie.

"Right. I'll give you two a minute," she replied, making a fast exit.

"How are you really doing?" Justice asked, leaning across the table and taking my hands into his.

I started to pull back simply from fear of how this all probably looked on camera, but I was too starved for human touch to deny myself this small pleasure.

"I'm keeping it together, trying to remain positive despite how bad shit looks."

"It'll never matter how bad shit looks because I'll be here through it all, and I damn sure ain't 'bout to leave you and my baby in here. How is our bundle of joy anyway?" he asked smiling.

"Fine, as far as they can tell. The nurses check on me twice a day, and I saw the doctor yesterday. She said we're both healthy."

"That's great news, baby! Don't worry, I'll have you back at the beach sipping non-alcoholic fruity drinks before you know it," he said smiling.

"How are things going out there with you?" I asked.

Immediately his expression changed and got darker.

"Pretty much the same."

I could feel that he wasn't being completely honest with me, but I understood it was because he probably didn't want to worry or stress me when I was already dealing with this shit.

"You need to go back to Oakland, don't you?" I asked.

"I'm exactly where I need to be, and my homies know that. Plus, it's good for me to be out of sight after what happened at the restaurant."

"Sounds like that situation might not be completely taken care of," I said nervously.

"Legally it is. There were no working cameras inside except at the cash register, and the shit happened too fast for anyone to get their phone out to record. Trust me, the cops ain't happy about that. Naturally there's even some backlash in the street, but nothing too serious because it's only speculation floating around and none of it is saying I pulled the trigger."

Somehow his explanation and reassurances didn't make me feel any better. What could I do though?

"I'ma need you to remember that you're supposed to be taking care of yourself out there because you've got a family to take care of," I said.

"Trust me, sweetheart, I'll never forget that," he replied, squeezing my hands and smiling at me.

"Don't smile at me like that because I need some dick."

"Well shit, don't let this table be what's stopping you from getting some," he said, leaning back in his chair.

"Right, and then I won't be able to see you again until God knows when. I can't go out like that."

Whatever he was planning to say was interrupted by the door opening behind me. I was expecting Stephanie to be coming back, but the way Justice's expression turned from sugar to shit signaled that it was someone else behind me.

"Time for your psych appointment, Dahl," Officer Lewellyn said.

I gritted my teeth to keep from spinning around and trying to pull his beard off his fucking face. It was more than difficult.

"When will you and Stephanie be back?" I asked, standing up.

"In a few days, unless something else comes up that can help us."

Hearing Lewellyn snickering behind me made me spin around fast with the intention of beating the white off him.

"EB," Justice said quickly.

The smirk on Lewellyn's face made it damn near impossible not to leap on him, but somehow I managed.

"Thought so. Now turn around," Lewellyn ordered, pulling his handcuffs out.

I reluctantly did as I was told, but when I saw the smile on Justice's face I felt my anger evaporate instantly. I mouthed the words *I love you*, and he nodded in agreement.

"You'll be out again, so just maintain. Oh, and Officer Lewellyn, I'll see you soon," he said, chuckling.

The fact that my handcuffs were put on without the extra added pressure from earlier told me that Officer Dick Face might finally have realized that he'd stepped in it now. When he turned me around to face him I gave him my brightest smile before stepping around him and out into the hallway. The pep in my step as I was led to the psychologist office obviously pissed Lewellyn off because he mumbled under his breath the entire way. I didn't give a fuck though, because I knew the odds were better than good that the clock to his life was ticking towards expiration at a rapid rate.

"Good afternoon, Dr. Phillips, how are you?" I asked, breezing into her office.

"I'm fine, Ebony, how are you?"

"The day is looking up, Doc," I replied, smiling.

Lewellyn had stopped mumbling, but that only lasted long enough to get my cuffs off because he was back to talking shit as he left the room. I took a seat across from the doctor and mentally prepared for the next round of chess.

"You seem to be in a social mood. Would you like to talk to me about that?" Dr. Phillips asked.

"Well, I just came from meeting with my lawyer, and she's working hard to get me out of here. I'm looking forward to that."

"I can imagine. Knowing your background, I know that this is probably the last place that you ever envisioned yourself being," she said.

"The run-in I had with my DUI was enough to scare me straight for damn sure."

"So have you asked yourself how you got here? And if you have, were you honest with yourself about the answer?" she asked.

"I know how I ended up in this situation," I replied quickly.

"How?"

Ivy's name was on the tip of my tongue, but I knew if I said that exactly where the conversation was headed. I had no doubt that we'd get around to discussing the triflin' bitch regardless, but I wasn't about to be backed into that corner like that.

"God's plan," I stated simply.

"God's plan? You accept that?"

"It's an indisputable fact that everything that has happened was supposed to happen. It's part of the grand design, and none of us possesses the wisdom to understand God's plan," I said.

"That's a very mature and interesting way to look at life, as well as the situation you've found yourself in. Most people that I've encountered in your position blame someone or something for why they are where they are in life."

"I don't see how that will help me grow," I said honestly.

"Very true. However, it's also true that God's plan is made up of many people and circumstances that are beyond your control, which means that *some* blame can be assigned to others. For instance, how you were raised heavily factors into your morals and values as you grow. How do you think

136

your parents would feel about what you've been accused of doing?" she asked.

For a moment I just stared at her, but I wanted to applaud her because this bitch was *good*. She'd taken what any normal person would interpret as my accepting where my life is right now, and spun that shit into the age old topic of parents and childhood! One thing I knew without a doubt was that she'd come to play, but I was far from a novice when it came to her kind and the mind fucking they liked to engage in. Her question only made me more determined to prove that. We spent the rest of our hour long session dueling like knights in the old days, jumping in and out of various subjects with the speed and precision of a sword thrust. By the time it was over, one thing was plainly clear to the good doctor. She had her hands full fucking with me.

"Ebony, I'd like to increase our sessions to twice a week starting next week."

"I guess if you feel that that's necessary, I won't waste time arguing," I replied.

"I must admit, given how our last session ended, I expected you to be more combative, especially on the topic of Ivy."

"Combative for what? I don't have to be ugly, aggressive, or disrespectful to tell you that she's alive because how I say it isn't gonna change whether you believe me or not," I said.

"Very true. Well, I look forward to our next session," she replied, standing to signal that we were done for the day.

I followed her lead and shook her hand before turning to signal escort. Surprisingly, when he put the cuffs back on me, he wasn't mumbling in the slightest. I started to instigate some shit, but I thought better of it and decided to keep my mouth shut as he led me back to my cell.

"Is that Dahl? I've got her dinner tray," a short Spanish chick said, walking towards where we stood outside my cell.

"Put it in there on her desk," Lewellyn instructed.

I'd been surprised to discover that the food here was edible, and I managed to choke most of it down.

"What's for dinner?" I asked her, nodding towards the tray in her hands.

"We made a special tray for you. Sinaloa revenge, puta!" she growled.

In a split second the tray disappeared, leaving only the razor in her grasp. Her swing was slow, but my reaction was slower. The blood came quick though.

Chapter 14
Ivy

"What are you doing?" Big asked calmly.

"Getting ready to eat. You wanna join us? I'm sure Juanito made enough," I replied.

"I did," Juanito confirmed, turning back to the pan on the stove.

Big looked from me to Juanito, and then back to me in silent evaluation. I knew my man, so I knew exactly what he was thinking, but to my way of thinking he had not a leg to stand on considering that another bitch had answered his phone.

"I'm not hungry," Big said.

"Did you eat while you were out with Star?" I asked sweetly.

This question made him narrow his eyes and tilt his head to the side as he continued staring at me.

"Are you being serious?" he asked.

"Do you want me to fix your plate, Ivy?" Juanito asked over his shoulder.

If he would've seen the look Big was levelling at him, he would've been reaching for his gun, but with his back to us, he was oblivious. It had been on the tip of my tongue to tell Big to come holla at me in another room, but getting a good look at his profile had me reaching for my own gun.

"I *know* you ain't crazy enough to come up in my house with another bitch's lipstick on your fucking collar," I said heatedly.

"Ivy, get that gun out of my face," Big said calmly.

"Or what, nigga?" I asked, cocking the hammer as my anger grew.

Quicker than I would've thought possible, Big smacked the barrel away from his face, causing me to accidentally pull the trigger and fire a wild shot. I felt the anger coursing through his body when he grabbed me by my throat and pulled me towards him roughly.

"Have you lost your mind?" he growled in my face.

"Take your hands off her," Juanito said calmly from behind me.

"This ain't got shit to do with you, Juanito. Stay out of it," Big replied, never taking his eyes off me.

For a second all I heard was Big breathing hard, but suddenly the metallic clicking of a pistol cocking echoed throughout the kitchen.

"I am not a man who repeats himself," Juanito said in the same calm tone.

Big's eyes flickered up and over my head, and then he let me go. Even as I was coughing and rubbing my throat, I couldn't believe that Big had actually snatched my little ass up. Then again, I couldn't believe that I'd pulled a gun on him. Despite all of that, though, I knew that shit was about to get way worse if I didn't step in and diffuse it.

"It's-it's okay, Juanito," I said, turning to him and waving for him to put the gun down.

My efforts didn't earn me so much as a glance. His focus, like his gaze, remained firmly fixed on Big. I tucked my pistol, took a step towards Juanito, and pushed the gun outstretched in his hand down to his side.

"I'm okay, Juanito," I reassured him.

When he looked at me, his stare was so intense that it felt like he had his hands on me, holding me firmly in place.

"I told you, we will protect our investment at all costs," he stated.

What he said was certainly an explanation as to why he'd been about to put a bullet in my husband, but the look in his eyes said more. They said things that I didn't wanna talk about.

"I'm fine, and thank you for cooking," I replied.

He nodded his head surely, taking my hint.

"I'll be in touch," he stated, staring pointedly at Big as he left.

When I turned back around, I was surprised to find three of James's men standing just behind Big with their guns out and matching looks of uncertainty about who was friend and who was foe.

"Everything is good, guys, my gun accidentally went off," I said, pulling the pistol back out to show them.

They nodded and made a quick exit behind Juanito, which left Big and I alone. Never in my life had things been this tense or awkward between us, and I didn't like it. I busied myself by putting my gun away and going to the stove to take the food off. I didn't know what else to do, so I made myself a plate of food and sat at the counter. Not surprisingly, Big was still standing in the same spot, and I could feel the heat from his stare trying to fuck up my perm.

"Where were you?" I asked around a mouthful of food.

"Fuck *all* that, I'ma need you to explain what the fuck just happened in here. I mean, I come home and you got Rico Suave cooking for you and shit, feeding you out of his goddamn hands, and then the nigga pulls a gun on me, to which you don't say or do shit!"

"I got him to lower it, didn't I? If you hadn't have put your hands on me like you'd lost your damn mind, none of that would've happened anyway," I said.

"Oh, I lost my damn mind? Not you for pulling a gun on my though right?"

"Don't show up with a bitch's lipstick on you," I replied, looking at him seriously.

"How about you try doing the adult thing and asking me maturely where the lipstick came from instead of getting on some bullshit? Don't let playing gangsta get you fucked up, bae, because I'm the real deal, and you and your bean eating partner ain't got no more chances to up the hammer on me. I promise you better drop that mu'fucka if you do."

I swallowed the ignorant shit I was about to say with another bite of food because I saw just how serious he was. Butting heads violently wasn't gonna get us anywhere, and it damn sure wasn't good for our child.

"You ain't never put your hands on me," I said.

"And I damn sure didn't ever intend to, but you didn't see the look in your eyes. The fact you fired off a wild shot should tell you how close you came to shooting me."

"If I ever found out that you fucked around on me, I would shoot you," I stated honestly.

Hearing this made him smile.

"Tell me something I *don't* know," he said, laughing softly.

"No, you tell *me* something I don't know. Where were you, and why did another bitch feel bold enough to answer your phone?"

"I was with the homies handling some petty bullshit, and if Star answered the phone, it was probably when I was shooting the fade with a nigga," he replied.

"The fade? Wait, you've been out fighting?" I asked, looking at him closer.

"You already know that sometimes all a mu'fucka respects is violence, but I'm good though."

"I see, not a mark on you, huh? That's good, but you still need to tell that bitch she's out of pocket for answering your phone, and she can have several seats. And you still need to explain that lipstick," I said, pointing at him with my fork.

"I went to see my grandmother since I missed her birthday while keeping vigil at your bedside."

"Oh," I replied sheepishly.

"It's your turn to answer questions, quick draw. For starters, where'd you get that pistol, because I know it's new," he said, grabbing a plate and filling it with food.

"Juanito gave it to me on behalf of him and Manuel."

I tried to make my answer sound nonchalant, but the way that he stared at me when he got across from me let me know that my goal wasn't achieved.

"Let me see it," he demanded.

I kept my expression neutral as I passed it to him. I continued eating while he gave it a thorough inspection before sitting it on the table in between us.

"I'd bet my left nut that that's real gold," he said.

I had to laugh at how serious his expression was.

"It ain't like they ain't got the money to do it," I acknowledged.

"Right, and the cost alone makes it an inappropriate gift to give another man's wife."

"Ah, so that's what your issue is? It's a sign of respect, that's all," I said.

He snorted in response and took a bite of his food. He immediately started shaking his head like he was tasting something that he didn't like.

"What?" I asked.

"The mu'fucka can cook too."

I laughed loudly at the pained expression on Big's face as he took another bite and chewed it slowly.

"This don't give him a pass for interfering in our domestic disagreement," Big stated.

"Duly noted, and I'll talk to him about that."

"What was he doing here anyway?" he asked.

"That's another topic entirely."

I quickly recapped everything for Big that he'd missed, including bringing him up to speed about Jeremy and his family.

"This mu'fucka Justice is really starting to get under my skin," Big declared.

"Tell me about it."

"We need to expedite our plans for Ebony. When is her preliminary court date?" he asked.

"I don't know. I'll find out though."

"To be honest I'm just ready to take some niggas and run up in the jail," he said.

I didn't have to ask if he was serious because I knew my nigga, and his crazy ass would be right there on the frontline with his homies.

"Somehow I don't think that's our play yet, baby," I said.

"Fuck all this cat and mouse shit because once we got what that nigga wants, we got him. You know like I do that he's not about to willingly lose child."

"You're right, but Juanito said the best thing to do was wait so that whatever move we make is proactive, and not simply a reaction to what Justice is doing," I said.

Big's stare was blank and his blinking was dramatically slow.

"Don't be an asshole, Big."

"I'm not. I'm just trying to figure out when Juanito's opinion mattered more than some two ply Charmin toilet paper," he replied.

"So you think what he said is wrong, or you know it's the right move, but you don't wanna admit it because he suggested it?"

"You're an asshole, Ivy."

"Exactly," I said, laughing and shaking my head at his bullshit.

The sound of voices headed in our direction halted our conversation and moments later, two teenage girls entered the kitchen.

"Alexa, Alexandra, it's been while," I said, smiling at the identical blond twins.

"At least two years, I think," Alexa said, coming around the counter to hug me.

Her sister followed her lead and then both sets of eyes immediately swung to my gun on the table. I quickly grabbed it and concealed it on me.

"I wish I was seeing you under better circumstances," I said honestly.

"It's so crazy because stuff like this just doesn't happen to people we know," Alexandra replied.

"I know, but nothing like that is gonna happen to either of you or your families," I vowed.

"Dad said that you would make sure of that. He said you're a serious bad ass now," Alexa said, smiling at me.

"Maybe a little," I admitted, laughing.

"You know we'll be eighteen in six months, so I don't think it would be a problem if you taught us how to shoot," Alexandra said.

Louis picked that exact moment to walk into the kitchen.

"We'll talk about that later, but for now, go make your-selves at home," I replied.

Both of them smiled, but didn't say anything as they turned and left.

"Ivy, thanks again," Louis said.

"Think nothing of it. I want you and your brother to get everybody situated, and then meet Big and I in the study."

"Okay," Louis replied, following his daughters.

"So everybody is staying here?" Big asked.

"Did I forget to mention that part? Well, I figured given the wall you built around our castle, and the added security, there is nowhere safer right now. Plus, your homies will be back down here," I reasoned.

"I got it. I don't like the idea of us having no privacy, especially given the fact we got some serious make-up sex to have, but I get it. I'll go make the necessary call to bring the soldiers home, and I'll meet you in the study."

I waited until he'd disappeared around the corner lead-ing outside before quickly grabbing his food and scrapping it onto my plate. I was gonna have to tell Juanito that I needed this recipe, after we talked about the awkward shit that had gone down today. Plate in hand, I made my way to my study, where I found Roger sitting in one of the chairs at my desk, staring off into space.

"You okay?" I asked gently, taking my seat.

"I just-I just keep seeing them."

"That's not something that you're likely to forget for a long time to come."

"You don't know who's behind it or why it happened? Unless you do know."

"Let's wait until everyone gets here before we have that conversation," I said, going back to my food.

He nodded his head and went back to his thoughts. A few minutes later Louis joined us, followed by Big.

"Did you seriously eat my food?" Big asked, closing the door behind him.

The empty plate sitting on the desk in front of me made lying impossible, so I gave him my sexiest smile.

"I love you, baby," I replied.

"Uh huh. First you try to kill me, and now you're trying to starve me?" Big asked.

"We can talk about that later. Right now we need to make sure we're all on the same page. Louis, Roger, I apologize for keeping the fact that I was alive a secret from you two. I want you to know that I didn't do it because I don't trust you," I said.

"I'm sure you had your reasons," Roger replied.

"I do, and you deserve to know what's going on because it all ties into what happened to Jeremy. I'll start with the good news first. I'm pregnant, and Big became my husband three weeks ago."

"Wow, you've been busy since faking your death," Louis said.

"Congratulations to you both. I know your dad would be happy for you," Roger said, smiling.

"Yeah, he would," I acknowledged, smiling at Big.

"Sadly, the reality still remains that Ebony and Justice are still problems that have to be dealt with," Big stated.

"You think they were behind what happened to Jeremy?" Roger asked.

"Well, Ebony is locked up, but I know it was Justice who killed Jeremy and his family. I'm almost positive that he believes I'm still alive, so he went after the link in our chain that he was familiar with to get information," I replied.

"But Jeremy didn't know you were alive. None of us did," Roger said.

"We know that, but Justice is fishing. I didn't anticipate him doing that, but we're prepared for it now and it's gonna be handled," Big said.

"I know that neither of you is interested in street politics, but I'm more than willing to lay out our plans if you want," I offered.

The brothers exchanged a look before Louis looked at me and nodded his head. I quickly outlined our play with Ebony and how we intended to flush Justice out. I made it clear that all I expected from them was to closely monitor all of our business ventures, because I couldn't afford to be distracted. With all of us being under the same roof, it would make things easier because we'd be working shoulder to shoulder. I offered them the room next to my office to set up shop in for practical reasons, but also for the sentimental one of having my dad's essence all around us. When the question of Jeremy's funeral service came up, I deferred to Louis and Roger's wishes because they'd been closer to Jeremy and his family. Plus, despite my want to pay my respects, I knew there was no way I could attend any type of service. Justice's suspicions hadn't been confirmed, and I was hoping that would make him doubt Ebony. By no means did I think that would make him leave her, but any chink in his armor was a plus for us. After bringing Louis and Roger up to speed, they excused themselves to give their families a sanitized version of what was happening, and what their plans were for the immediate future.

"Lock the door," I instructed once Big and I were alone.

He didn't need to ask me why because I was already pulling my shirt over my head, giving him an unobscured view of my firm titties.

"I'm not gonna be gentle with you," he warned, moving away from the door towards me with a hunger bordering starvation clouding his eyes.

"Don't talk about it, be about it."

This time when his hand went around my throat, the only part of me that panicked was my pussy, pounding with anticipation and need. I only got my shorts halfway down over my hips before I was spun around and bent over my desk.

My phone ringing was the last thing we needed, but that didn't silence it. Big was nice enough to reach into my shorts pocket, grab it, and pass it to me, but I could tell he was still completely focused on our making up.

"Hel-lo!" I moaned, answering the phone as Big shoved his dick in me with savage force.

"It's me."

I wanted to tell Angelique that this was way beyond bad timing, but if she was calling me now, then it was with an update because technically she was still on the clock as Doctor Phillips.

"Uh huh," I replied, trying to brace myself with one arm while Big dove into the deep end of my pool fast and hard.

"We have a problem," she said.

"P-problem! What-what problem?" I asked.

"I'm not stopping," Big vowed.

To prove his point he grabbed my hips with both hands and fucked me with long, steady strokes.

"Ebony was attacked, and she got slicked up pretty bad. She's at the hospital," Angelique said.

"O-okay. Thank-thank you," I replied breathlessly.

"There's more. There's an officer suspected of letting it happen, and her lawyer was already asking for bail. The general consensus is that she's gonna get it now," Angelique informed me.

"Fuck!" I exclaimed, cumming hard enough to make me drop my phone.

It was ten minutes before Big paused long enough to let me grab it, but by then, Angelique was gone and all that was left was opportunity.

Chapter 15
Ebony
One day later

The tears cascading down my face weren't a result of the pain that I was feeling, at least not completely. What hurt more than the pain of the staples holding my cheek together and the stiches I'd gotten on both hands was the knowledge that I would forever be scarred. I hadn't thought that I was particularly vain, especially given the adjustments I'd made to my way of living when I'd agreed to stay with Justice in Oakland. Having my face permanently disfigured was something completely different though. They'd had to sedate me when I'd been brought into the emergency room in order to operate, so I hadn't gotten a chance to talk to any doctor about anything. I'd awoken to hear the news that my surgery had been a success, but I'd have an ugly scar that went from my left ear to the left corner of my mouth. At first I'd thought my scar would be just a line that, once healed, I'd be able to cover up with make-up. The doctor had just given me the harsh truth a few minutes ago that because of how deeply I'd been sliced, and the fact that staples had to be used, my scar would be big and puffy. There was no concealing it.

"Ms. Dahl, your lawyer and paralegal are here," a cop said, sticking his head inside the door to my hospital room.

"Okay," I replied, wiping the tears from the right side of my face. I didn't have to worry about the left side since there was a mountain of bandaging there that could absorb wetness.

The cop disappeared and seconds later, Justice came through the door, followed closely by Stephanie. Neither of them spoke a word, but Justice quickly moved to my side and took me into his arms. It hadn't been my intention to cry, but being in the security of his arms released all my inhibitions, and I bawled like a baby.

"It's okay, I'm here," he said soothingly.

I just cried. I don't know how long I cried, but it was only pure exhaustion that forced me to stop.

"Here, drink this," he instructed, passing me the cup of orange juice that had been sitting on my tray table.

I took a couple of sips despite the discomfort that came from drinking, and then I passed him the cup back.

"I need you to tell me what happened, Ebony," Stephanie said, pulling out a hand held recorder.

"I was-I was coming back from my session with Doctor Phillips and there was a girl in the hallway. She said she had a tray for me, and Officer Lewellyn told her to put it in my cell. I asked her what was on the tray, and the next thing I know she's coming at me with a blade."

"What did you do?" Stephanie asked.

"The first blow was unexpected so I couldn't do anything, but when I saw my blood flying, my adrenaline kicked in and I was able to slip my cuffs in time to get my hands up," I replied.

"Officer Lewellyn is saying that you slipped your cuffs first and made an aggressive move towards the female. Her name is Rosalinda Flores," Stephanie said.

"If I'd slipped my cuffs first, do you really think I would've allowed that bitch to do this to my face?" I asked heatedly.

"Calm down, baby, she's only telling you what the official report says, but it's clear that it's bullshit," Justice said, holding me tighter.

"What did the cameras catch?" I asked.

The look on Stephanie's face said it all before she opened her mouth.

"Maintenance still hadn't fixed the ones on your walk yet," she replied.

"Right, because if they would've done that, they might've seen Ivy's sneaky ass lurking around," I said, disgusted.

"You saw Ivy again?" Justice asked quickly.

"No, I'm just saying that there's no such thing as coincidence. I mean, it's obvious that she has the Fort Worth police department in her back pocket after all she killed a mu'fucka in the parking lot outside the police station and got away with it. Orchestrating a hit on me while I'm in their custody is child's play," I replied, getting angrier at the helpless feeling growing inside me.

"Well, I think that she overplayed her hand because this whole situation was slopping in planning and execution. It's so obvious that Officer Lewellyn was a part of this, and that works to your advantage," Stephanie said.

"How so?" I asked.

"Because I've already spoken to the judge, and all we're waiting on is the official order signed granting you house arrest," Stephanie replied smiling.

"I'm-I'm getting out of jail?" I said in shock and disbelief.

"Yep, you and my baby are coming home," Justice said.

Hearing this had tears streaming down my face for a different reason. I knew that I'd still have to face my case in court, but at least now I had options with regards to where I had my baby. The most important thing to me was securing my little one's future.

"I don't know how you pulled this miracle off, but thank you, Stephanie," I said sincerely.

"Well, the fact that you're in the hospital after being assaulted helped a lot. If you or your baby would've died while you were in police custody, the press would've had a field day kicking the department's ass! This might even get you some sympathetic jurors, provided that you don't run," she replied, giving me a knowing look.

I decided to move right on past that subject entirely.

"Wait, I don't have a house to go to out here. Ivy destroyed those," I said, looking at Justice.

"I took care of that when I first came back out here and Stephanie told me there was a possibility for house arrest. It's safe," he replied, sliding his hand under my gown and resting it on my stomach.

"Can you put my trial off until after I give birth?" I asked.

"I'm confident that I can, but you're gonna have to continue with your psychologist sessions," Stephanie replied.

I wasn't excited about this, but I knew what the end game was so there was no way that I was about to complain.

"Okay, so when can we leave?" I asked, looking back to Justice.

"I'll go see if the order has come down," Stephanie said, leaving us alone.

As soon as the door closed, Justice's mouth attacked mine quicker than that little Spanish bitch had, but I didn't fight against him. I knew that he was trying to be gentle because of my face, but it had been so long since I'd had something as simple as this that I ignored the pain, determined to lose myself in him. When the hand that he'd had on my stomach slid down and into my panties, my breath got trapped in my lungs, but him working my clit allowed me to exhale.

"Come here," I demanded, trying to pull him all the way in the bed with me.

"We'll do all that later. Just relax for now," he insisted.

I wanted to argue, but the rhythmic dance of his fingers had my vision swimming in and out of focus already. His kisses kept my sounds of hunger and need between us, and a couple minutes later, my climax melted me in his arms.

"I-I need more," I confessed, again trying to coax him into the bed.

"Patience, baby."

I knew that the pout on my face was sexy, but he simply chuckled and shook his head as he licked my juices off of his fingers.

"Believe me, I want you right now, but we need to keep my cover as your paralegal intact. As soon as I get you home, though, you best believe your whole ass is mine," he said passionately.

I didn't know if his statement or the aftershocks from my orgasm made me tingle more. I just knew that I was gonna act a fool when we got behind closed doors.

"So let me ask you something. Besides the obvious, why do you think it was Ivy?" he asked seriously.

"Because I lied to Stephanie when I implied that the bitch who attacked me didn't say anything. She said something about this being revenge from Sinaloa."

"I thought Ivy was fucking with the Gulf Cartel," Justice said.

"Right, but if she turned the tape of me killing Esteban's nephew over to the cops, why wouldn't she give it to the Sinaloa Cartel too? That's just one more person to do her bidding and come after us," I replied.

"I don't know, EB. I mean, it makes sense, but I don't get Ivy putting together that type of strategic move. Maybe Big, but not her."

"Have you learned nothing from understanding that bitch?" I asked, feeling frustration contort my facial features.

"Okay, so let's say that was her play. I hate to admit it, but I think you were right when you said that we need to run. I ain't no bitch, but I don't see how we win against two cartels and the Hoovers, especially because your house arrest means we gotta stay in Texas. At this point, it's suicide," he said, shaking his head.

I knew just how hard it was for him to accept defeat, but I knew he was man enough to know his pride wasn't worth more than me or our baby.

"Did I have to forfeit my plane as part of the deal to get house arrest?"

"Yeah, but that's okay because that was just a way for them to track your movements. I know how to move around below the radar, but we're gonna burn a lot of money," he warned.

"So what? As soon as you get me home, I'm gonna move every dollar that I can far beyond the government reach because once they know I'm in the wind, they're gonna seize what they can. I've already moved a lot, but I'm gonna liquidate everything."

"Do you have a preference on where we spend forever?" he asked.

The truth was that I did know where I wanted to go because I'd spent countless hours daydreaming about running far and fast. For the life of me, I couldn't remember any of the plans I'd made though because my mind was completely consumed by what Justice was holding in his hand.

"Wh-what?" I asked weakly.

"I asked if you know where you want to spend forever, and this ring right here is a symbol of the forever I had in mind," he replied, pulling the sparkling diamond from the box.

The sudden fear that gripped me was paralyzing because I thought that he intended to take my wedding ring off of my finger and replace it with his engagement ring. I didn't wanna hurt his feelings, but if he touched my ring that Rockafella had given me, I knew I was gonna snap.

"J-J, wait, I - "

I closed my mouth when he slid the ring in his hand onto my right ring finger and kissed it.

"I know that you're not over losing Rock, and I'm in no way trying to force you to forget him or stop grieving for him. I just want you to know that there's definitely sunshine after the rain, but for now we'll stand out in the storm together. I'm not going anywhere," he vowed, leaning down and kissing me on the forehead.

I had no idea what the fuck I was supposed to say in this moment, but I was praying that Stephanie would come save me. I knew my tears would buy me a little time, allowing me to organize my thoughts and figure out how to navigate the land mines of emotions between us.

"J, you know that I love you, but it wouldn't be fair for me to marry you right now. I'm an emotional hot-ass mess."

"I get that. But you should know that none of that stops me from loving you, or from being here for you. When we get married isn't as important as you knowing that I'll always be here, and that one day we will get married. Baby, it's really you, me, and our child against the world," he declared sincerely.

"Okay," I said, accepting what he was saying and offering.

"Okay? So that means…"

"That means you're stuck with me, so I hope you know what you're getting yourself into," I replied, smiling.

"Oh, don't worry, I'm familiar with you and all your bullshit, sweetheart. I can handle it. Now, are you gonna tell me where we're going?"

I didn't have a chance to reply because the door was suddenly opened, and we quickly scrambled to look professional.

"Ms. Dahl, it's time for me to change your bandage," Nurse Macy said, coming into the room.

I was reluctant to let go of Justice's hand, but I did it so that the short brunette could handle her business. I felt so self-conscious, but Justice smile at me genuinely the whole time the nurse was changing the bandage, and putting more ointment in my face and hands. Once Macy was done, she left us alone, and Justice immediately took my hand again.

"You sure you're gonna want to wake up to this face every day?" I asked.

"Are you serious?"

"Yeah, I'm serious. I know I'm ugly now, so - "

"Shut up with all that shit you wasting your breath on because you'll never be ugly. The scar you're gonna have is only gonna make you more beautiful, and I didn't think that was possible. You ain't never been the insecure type,

158

so don't change up now because I ain't going for it. Understand?" he asked seriously.

I nodded my head, unable to suppress the smile tugging at my lips. The door opened again, but this time it was Stephanie returning.

"I hope that smile on your face translates into good news for me," I said, looking at her closely.

"I do come with good news. The order is signed, but we're still waiting on it to be entered into the system so that the jail knows you're no longer in their custody. Don't worry though, you're not in any danger of being transported back to the jail in between now and when the order goes in. I spoke to the chief of police and he's only too happy to have you gone," Stephanie replied.

"So how long are we looking at?" Justice asked.

"No more than a couple hours," she said, looking at the watch on her wrist.

"A'ight, that gives me time to handle a few things," he said, kissing me on the top of my head before moving towards the door.

"J?" I said.

"Don't worry, EB, I'll be back before you know it."

He flashed me his most mischievous smile, and then he was gone.

"He loves you," Stephanie said.

"Yeah, I know, that's not what worries me."

"Ah. Well, there are some papers that you have to sign, and my associate is bringing them to us here. In the meantime, I want you to get a full physical so that anything that's wrong can be documented while you're still in police custody," she said.

"Sounds like a plan."

It was only the beginning, though, because the real plans involved ensuring the life of me, Justice, and my baby. Our baby.

"I need you to do something for me, Stephanie, but it has to stay between us. Not even Justice can know."

"Okay. It sounds serious," she replied slowly.

"I won't lie to you, it is. It's a matter of life and death, and its more than one life hanging in the balance."

Chapter 16
Ivy

My sleep was dreamless and relaxing, and having it interrupted by my phone ringing had me all the way pissed off before I reached blindly for it on my night stand.

"Somebody better fucking be dead," I said, answering with my eyes still closed.

"The judge approved her house arrest."

Hearing the news came from the mouth of Chief Stringer forced my eyes open so that I could look at the clock to see what time it is.

"Is that official in the system yet?" I asked.

"Not yet. I did a few things to delay it until I could let you know what was going on. I tried to get in touch with Big, but he didn't answer his phone."

I looked next to me, but the spot Big slept in was empty, and the sheets were cool to my touch. Knowing my husband, he was probably out by the pool smoking a blunt or something. At least his ass better be doing something that innocent at 1 a.m. since he wasn't in the bed beside me sleeping.

"Is she still at the hospital?" I asked.

"Yeah, but everything is in place for her to walk out at any moment. She already has the ankle monitor on, and her temporary P.O. has done a home visit too."

"Where the fuck is she going? She don't have a house out here," I said, surprised by how swiftly this bitch had lined everything up. Money definitely moved mountains, but she obviously had help spending it.

"Justice got the house a few days after she was locked up, and it's in Dallas."

This made sense because he had homies out there. That meant that I needed to make my move now before he barricaded them in like he had in Oakland.

"A'ight, I'll take care of it," I replied, hanging up.

I quickly climbed out of bed and threw on some shorts and a T-shirt before going in search of Big. It only took me five minutes to realize that he wasn't in the house, and the fact that his car wasn't in the driveway meant he wasn't anywhere on the grounds.

"*Not* the time for this shit," I mumbled, dialing his number.

The fact that his phone just kept ringing only added to my frustration, and before I knew it, I was out the front door, headed towards the front gate.

"What time did my husband leave?" I asked the two young white guys sitting in the tiny booth. I could tell that I'd startled them, but they played it off well by pulling out the handwritten log they kept and quickly comparing notes.

"Midnight," Matt replied, looking at his watch before looking at me.

"Thanks," I said, turning and heading back to the house.

I tried to call Big two more times before sending him a text message telling him to get his ass home *now*! I waited ten minutes before I said fuck it and texted Juanito to let him know what the situation was and what I needed. A few minutes later he hit me back, surprising me by telling me that he'd sent some of his men to the hospital, and he was on his way to get me. I immediately typed him a response, letting him know that I appreciated him putting his men on it, but it was a bad idea for him to come pick me up. I didn't send it though. Instead, I erased that message, typed "ok", and went to change clothes. I threw on an all-black sweat suit, tucked my hair under a black stocking cap, grabbed my new .45, and was out the door.

Ten minutes later, Juanito slid to a stop in front of the gate in his 2021 black-on-black E85 AMG Mercedes.

"I can tell that I didn't wake you up because you got here fast," I said, sliding into the passenger seat.

"I like to work at night, so I rarely sleep before sunrise. Where's Big?"

I know that he probably had logical reasons for asking that question, but not knowing the answer pissed me off more.

"I don't know," I replied shortly.

Without a word, he pulled off into the night. Outside of Ebony and my father, there had never been anyone I discussed Big with, but for some reason, I felt comfortable with Juanito.

"He's probably out handling business. I got the call about Ebony, and it woke me up, so I didn't even know that he wasn't home. Its time sensitive though," I said.

"I agree. Justice has a way of shielding himself when he's in a familiar environment. I would admire it if I wasn't determined to kill him."

"I appreciate your determination," I said genuinely.

"I know that you'll kill if you have to, but for the most part, you're about business so you understand how an on-going war hurts business. I appreciate your determination to get this shit over with so that we can get back to making money. And I apologize if I overstepped the other day."

I knew that this would have to be addressed eventually, and I was glad that we were alone to have this conversation.

"I understand why you did what you did, but it made shit awkward," I confessed.

"I understand. I'm not sorry that I got involved when he put his hands on you, but I could've done it without pulling my gun."

"Right. I mean, I respect why you felt the need to step in, but I actually thought you were gonna shoot Big," I said.

"I was," he replied, looking over at me.

I wasn't sure what I was supposed to say to that, so I didn't say shit. Instead, I pulled my phone out and tried to call Big again. No answer after endless rings had me doing some shit that I swore I wouldn't do. Since I was the one who bought the car he was out cruising in, I had direct access to his GPS, so I took a peek to see where exactly my nigga was.

"Can you check with your people and find out if there's been any movement at the hospital?" I asked.

Without a word, he pulled out his phone and made the call, speaking in rapid Spanish. While he did, that I sent James a text, instructing him to meet me at the address I was sending him.

"Ebony is still in the hospital. The cops are still there, but so are some people who don't blend in well enough to be a part of the staff," Juanito informed me.

"Justice's people, probably."

"I've added to my numbers, but I should warn you that this is probably gonna get ugly," he said.

"In more ways than one. I need you to make a detour to this address," I replied, passing him my phone.

He looked at it briefly before passing it back to me.

"Type it into my car's GPS."

I did what he told me, and he pointed us in the right direction. A few minutes later, I got a response from James telling me that he was on the way.

"You're not gonna ask why we're going to this address?" I asked.

"Do you want me to ask?"

"I just assumed that you'd want to know what type of shit I was getting you into," I replied.

"Not really. I believe that your personal decisions are made with the same ruthless calculation as your business decisions, so whatever we're doing is more than likely necessary."

I wished it was as easy as he put it, but emotional moves were never anything less than complicated.

"I'm pregnant," I blurted out.

As soon as I spoke those words, there was a very loud voice in my mind that yelled "Oh shit!" I had no idea why I'd just told him that because it damn sure hadn't been my intention.

"Does Big know?"

"Of course. Why would you ask me that?" I asked, looking over at him.

"Because I was wondering if he knew that when he grabbed you by your throat," Juanito replied.

Even in the darkness, I could see his facial features tighten in anger.

"He-he wasn't gonna hurt me. I just overreacted to seeing lipstick on his collar."

"Overreacted, huh? Is that why we're making a slight detour on our way to handle important business?" he asked, looking at me.

I didn't see judgment in his eyes, but I was still unsettled because I felt like he was looking through me.

"The bottom line is that Big wouldn't hurt me, and he knows that I'm pregnant."

"How far along are you?" he asked.

"Three months."

"Congratulations," he said, reaching over and squeezing my hand.

Despite his anger, I knew that his well wishes were sincere, and I took comfort in that. When he didn't pull his hand away from mine, I got worried though. Not because we were holding hands, but because I wasn't trippin' that we were holding hands. My rationale was that friends could hold hands, although I was struggling to remember exactly when we'd became friends. He didn't move his hand, and I didn't make him, so that's how we arrived at our destination fifteen minutes later.

Big's cotton candy blue Phantom wasn't hard to spot, especially in this middle class suburb, but Juanito did the smart thing and eased to the curb a couple houses away from where Big was parked. I sent James a text letting him know that we were here, and a few seconds later, the high beams on his Range Rover flashed one time from the other end of the block.

"Is this an official stakeout, like in the movies?" Juanito asked, smiling.

"Not hardly. Once I have enough facts pointing at an indisputable truth, we can leave," I replied, texting James again.

"And what truth is that?"

"That my husband is doing something he shouldn't be," I replied, looking towards the house Big's car was parked in front of.

There were no lights on anywhere, not even some illumination from the flickering of a TV, which gave the impression that everyone inside was asleep. My nigga ain't have no business sleeping anywhere except at home in our bed, so now the real question was how I wanted to handle this.

"What are you thinking?" Juanito asked.

"That if my dad were alive, he'd tell me that the only things open this late were IHOP and legs."

My response made him laugh in a deep, rich tone that gave me chills.

"Seems like your dad was wise in many areas of life, but I meant what are you thinking about this situation," he said.

The phone vibrating in my hand provided me with information that changed my thought process.

"We can leave. My security is gonna stay here and watch," I replied, sending another text.

"Aren't your security people best served at your side?"

"Not right now. Right now I need answers, plus I'm safe with you," I said, looking over at him.

"Yes, you are," he stated, starting the car and pulling off.

Despite my ability to talk to Juanito, I stayed in my own thoughts, searching for a way out that wouldn't leave me broken or scarred deeply. The preliminary evidence was this: Big wasn't at home where he should be, this wasn't his first time ghosting without an explanation beforehand, and the house he was at was owned by a female named Starmel Brown. I had no doubt that people called her Star for short. All of that added up to Big fucking around on me, which brought me in a full circle to the same damn question. What was I gonna do about it?

"Juanito, can I ask you something?"

"Sure," he replied.

"Why do men cheat?"

"For a number of reasons. Some do it because they have insecurity issues that make them sabotage a good or normal relationship. For others, it can be an addiction like any other thing that brings you pleasure. Some men cheat because they can though, because they have the ability to seduce women and that gives them a false sense of power," he replied honestly.

"Have you ever cheated?" I asked.

"No."

His response and the speed with which it was delivered had me looking at him sideways, which made him laugh again.

"I can tell that you don't believe me, but I've never cheated because I would never have to. I've always been up front with a woman about any other woman I was sleeping with."

"Ah, I see. So you're a playboy, not the marrying type," I said, nodding my head.

"For the right woman I would definitely settle down and cherish her forever."

The way he looked at me when he spoke those words instantly reminded me that I didn't have any panties on, and that made me ask myself why? Why hadn't I put my panties on?

"Are you seeing anybody now?" I asked softly, avoiding eye contact by looking out the window at the night around us.

"Not currently, no. I'm waiting for the right person."

I knew that I was walking on dangerous ground, but I didn't care right now. Undoubtedly I'd care later, but not right now. I casually leaned over and punched another destination into his GPS, only glancing briefly before relaxing in the comforts of his passenger seat. He didn't speak a word, but it only took a few minutes for me to realize that he was taking me where I wanted to go. Ten minutes later he stopped the car, and I got out.

"This place looks familiar," he said, joining me in front of the car. His headlights blazed a bright path out across the field, startling some of the nocturnal creatures that called this place home.

"Ebony and I use to call this our field of dreams when we used to play here as kids. Since then I come here whenever I need to think or just get away, but most recently it was the site where Esteban's nephew met his end."

"Ah. I'm surprised that the police haven't put up barriers to prevent people from coming back here," he said, looking around.

"It would be hard for them to do that considering that I own the land."

"Of course you do," he replied, smiling at me.

"You're too damn pretty to be as deadly as you are," I blurted out, shaking my head in slight disbelief.

Of course this made him laugh, but just as quickly the laughter died in his throat and he pulled me tightly against him.

"You're too beautiful to be unappreciated," he whispered seductively.

I had no response to his words, and even if I did, it wouldn't have mattered because his lips were suddenly on mine. He kissed me like he knew me, like we'd been doing this for years and years instead of this being our first time. Our tongues danced together with an effortless grace that contained unspeakable chemistry. I could literally feel my pussy juices running down my thighs, and he hadn't even touched me yet. When he pulled my gun from the small of my back I did the same to his, and both of them ended up on the car. Next came our clothes, leaving us completely naked in the moonlight, but the feeling of his hands on me kept me warm despite the cool breeze.

"You're so gorgeous," he said, looking me over from head to toe.

"So are you," I replied, running my hands down his chest until I came into contact with his dick.

When he scooped me up in his arms, I thought that he was gonna put me on the hood of the car, but instead he led me down in the grass on top of our clothes. The glare of the headlights illuminated the work of art that was his body, but the fact that he was kissing his way down my body made it hard to concentrate. His lips and tongue attacked my clit like sworn enemies, and then quickly made up like lovers do. Somehow my hands ended up in his hair, gripping his curls while he made my back defy gravity.

"Oh shit, Juan-Juan-i-to," I moaned.

Each flicker of his tongue pushed the darkness away until I saw daylight in the form of an orgasm that left me breathless. When he moved back up my trembling body and kissed me again, I could taste my pussy all over his tongue, and it turned me on as much as him gently pushing his dick inside me. I was beyond wet, but I was tight enough to have him shaking as he submerged himself in me. It took him a couple minutes to get his sea legs, but once he got used to me, his strokes hit me with the force of dynamite. The fact that he was whispering in my ear in Spanish took the moment from sexy to erotic, and we never looked back. Right as my second orgasm peeked from behind the clouds, my phone started ringing. Juanito paused, but I quickly wrapped my legs around him and pulled him deeper into my dungeon.

"It can wait," I said, lifting into pounding blows as he moved faster.

Moments later we came together loudly, but Juanito only stopped long enough to turn me over. I thought he was gonna pull me up on all fours, but instead he kept me pinned to the ground with long, slow strokes. It felt so good that I couldn't get a word out of my mouth, I could only moan my pleasure to the night.

Suddenly both our phones were ringing, but cumming was our only concern. It felt like his dick was growing inside me with every stroke, making me fear that he was gonna forever damage the walls on this kitty. I didn't care though. I squeezed his dick until I felt him surrender his seed to me, and then I came again. The fact that our phones hadn't stopped ringing didn't allow us any time to cuddle, but it also prevented the awkward transition from what had just happened. Once he got off me, I rolled off our clothes, passing him his phone while I answered mine. I was trying to focus on the update from James, but I could hear the sound of gunshots coming from Juanito's phone.

"I'll call you back," I said, hanging up.

Juanito's call ended just as quickly.

"We gotta go, shit just got crazy," he said, passing me my gun back.

Aryanna

Chapter 17
Ebony

"We've got a problem," Justice said softly, quickly crossing from the door to my bedside.

"What is it?" I asked, dread filling me as I anticipated him saying that the judge had changed his mind.

"Well, in order for the ankle monitor that you've got on to work, we have to have a regular land line and not a cell phone. The phone company hasn't gotten around to hooking the one up at the house yet, and you can't leave until they do."

"So-so I gotta go back to jail?" I asked, trying not to get emotional over the prospect.

"No, baby, I'm not going for that. I offered him twenty thousand dollars to get it done tonight, or there would be another alternative that he didn't want to face. He assured me that it would be done, but it means we've gotta sit here a little longer, and I know that you're ready to get the fuck out of here."

"Yeah, I am, but if the worst case scenario is that I'm stuck here for a little while longer, I can deal with that. I just don't wanna go back to jail," I said adamantly.

"Trust me, I'm not letting you go that easy. Are you hungry?" he asked, sitting on the bed next to me.

"Yeah, but I want some real food, not this hospital shit. It's almost as bad as the jail."

"Yeah, I know. So if you could have anything to eat, what would it be?" he asked.

"Honestly, I want a really good hamburger. Not from a fast food chain, but like a burger you get at a bar," I replied, licking my lips.

"If you could see the expression on your face right now."

I moved to hit him for laughing at me, but the last thing that I needed was to open up the stitches in my hands.

"Fuck you, Negro! You know that the jail food ain't shit, and I'm pregnant, so I'm craving good quality food," I said defensively.

"I know, and I got you. Hit your call button real quick."

For a moment I simply looked at him because I was sure that his ass was up to no good, and I didn't wanna get in no trouble that could fuck up my house arrest. At least not before I got out of police custody.

"Justice - "

"EB, just hit the call button, it's not that serious," he said, smiling.

I hit the button, and a few minutes later, Macy came into the room.

"Everything okay, Ms. Dahl?" she asked.

"Actually, it's not, Nurse," Justice replied.

"What's wrong?" Macy asked, moving to my side so that she could get a good look at me and the monitors beeping steadily.

"Well, you see, she's pregnant, and hungry, and I'm sure that you've probably seen all types of shit go wrong when that combination of events is not handled properly," Justice said seriously.

Macy laughed while nodding her head. "Are you craving something specific?" she asked.

"A burger from a bar," I replied sheepishly.

"Ah, well, you're in luck because I know just the place," Macy said, smiling.

Justice quickly pulled two one hundred dollar bills from his pocket and handed them to the nurse.

"Bring back two," he instructed.

"Okay, but they don't cost that much," she said.

"Consider the extra a tip for fast delivery," he replied.

"I'll be back before you know it," she said, pocketing the money and heading out the door.

"Thanks, babe," I said, pulling him towards me for a quick kiss.

"You're more than welcome. You know that I can't have you and my baby starving."

"Speaking of the baby, there's something that I need to talk to you about," I said seriously.

"Okay, what is it?"

"I want you to sign the birth certificate," I replied.

"You mean after the DNA test and - "

"No, I mean when the baby is born, I want you to sign the birth certificate because you're the father regardless. We don't need a DNA test," I said confidently.

"Are you-are you sure, bae?"

"I'm positive," I replied, smiling at him.

I could see the wide range of emotions moving across his face, none of which was suspicions about my real motivations. I knew that Justice wouldn't be able to handle it if the child I was carrying wasn't his, at least not in the long run. It would be stupid of me to wait on that shoe to drop out of the sky and crush me. So I went on the offensive by making this decision, but I also had a DNA test secretly done with my lawyer being the only one who had access to the results. It truly didn't matter what the truth was because the favor I'd asked of Stephanie was to have test results manufactured that said Justice was the father. Only me, Stephanie, and God would know what the complete truth was if Justice wasn't biologically my child's father.

He put his hand on my stomach while kissing me passionately. As our kiss deepened, I could feel his hand taking the familiar path down into my panties, but I stopped him and pulled back.

"No playing. You're either gonna fuck me or leave me alone," I stated seriously.

His indecision was easy to interpret and I thought that my ultimatum would get me what I wanted, but I was left disappointed as he reluctantly backed away.

"Ohhh, you're sooo gonna pay for making we wait," I vowed, chuckling mischievously.

"You do realize that you're threatening me with a good time, right? I know your pussy like the back of my hand, and I know how to swim."

"Maybe you do know my pussy. What about my head game though?" I asked, licking my lips suggestively while looking him directly in the eyes.

"I can-I can handle that too," he replied, fighting the cracking in his voice.

I laughed at him because I could see that he wasn't confident at all. I had no doubt that I could make him cum in under two minutes flat. I teased him about this very real probability until Macy returned ten minutes later with a greasy brown paper bag in her hand. Before she crossed the room, I smelled the delicious burger, grilled onions, melted cheese, pickles, and French fries.

"Oh God, Macy, I think that I love you," I said, holding my hands out for the food.

"Wait until you taste it," she replied.

"You eat. I'll be right back. I'm gonna check on everything," Justice said, winking at me as he moved out of the way so that Macy could push the tray table up to me.

"Hurry back," I said, blowing him a kiss.

Macy quickly unpacked the food and that became my sole focus in life.

"These burgers are huge, and you got three of them! There's no way that I can eat all of this," I said, shaking my head.

"Trust me, once you taste it you'll damn sure be willing to try."

"No, I want you to eat this one," I insisted, pushing one of the burgers at her.

I could tell she was about to argue, but I held up my hand because I didn't have time to hear it. I unwrapped my burger and dove head first on that mu'fucka, closing my eyes in pure ecstasy at the taste of it.

"Yeah, I *definitely* love you, Macy," I whispered, chewing slowly.

"Amazing, right?"

"I can't even put it into words, but thank you," I replied sincerely.

"Oh, you're welcome, but I should really be thanking you."

"Believe me, this food is worth more than two hundred dollars. In fact - "

"No, that's not what I meant. I mean I appreciate your generosity, but I would've done it for free if you would've asked," she said, talking softer.

"Really?"

"Of course. So would have a few other nurses that work here. You're a hero to us," she stated seriously.

"A hero? I don't think so. You've probably got me confused with somebody else."

"No, it was you who killed that cartel hitman. The cartels have ruined so many lives, and we have to see it because we work here at the hospital. We're sick of it! But we love the fact that you stood up to the bully and drew blood, kinda like in that movie *300*. You've demonstrated that a God-king can bleed," she said, smiling at me.

Her smile was infectious, and before I knew it, she had me laughing like we were two girlfriends from high school, sharing a meal and catching up. I couldn't remember the last time that I'd had such innocent fun, and the look on Justice's face when he came back through the door made me wonder when I'd know fun again. He came with a cop in tow, but there was nothing left of our meal except trash in a bag, so I wasn't worried about getting caught. The cop didn't say shit anyway. He simply stepped to the side of my bed, unhooked the handcuff from my left wrist, and put the cuffs in his pocket.

"You're officially not my problem," he declared, leaving the room as quickly as he'd come.

"So does this mean you're free?" Macy asked.

"Not hardly, but it's a start," I replied, still trying to read Justice's expression.

"Can you make sure that all of her discharge paperwork is in order?" Justice asked.

"Of course. I'll be right back," Macy said, disappearing out the door.

"What's wrong?" I asked immediately.

"We've got company outside, maybe even in the hospital."

"Okay, well, you kinda expected that didn't you?" I asked immediately.

"Yeah, but not like this. My homies said they couldn't spot everyone, but they went from feeling like they had the upper hand to being seriously outnumbered," he replied, clearly frustrated.

"O-okay, so what's the plan?"

"Well, the way I figure it is that whoever is out there is simply waiting on the cops to leave so that they can attack. If we're as outnumbered as my homies believe, then we're sitting fucking ducks," he stated.

"Okay. So what's the plan?" I asked slower, hoping that bad news wasn't all he'd brought back with him.

He quickly pulled a Sig Sauer 9mm from the waist of his suit pants and passed it to me.

"It's loaded and the safety is off. The plan is that as soon as the cops get ready to leave, my people are gonna start dumping shots at the threats that they can identify. Naturally the cops will get included and call for back up, which is gonna turn the parking lot into a shit show."

"And a much-needed distraction," I said, swinging my feet to the floor.

"Yeah, a much-needed distraction, and it'll be happening any minute, so you need to get dressed *now*."

After setting the gun on the bed, I quickly grabbed the bag in the corner that he'd brought me with my clothes in it. I put on my jeans, T-shirt, sneakers, and hoody before grabbing the pistol off the bed and tucking it into my jeans.

"I'm assuming that we're not going out of the front door," I said.

"Nope, we're gonna - "

His sentence was interrupted by the sound of gunfire. It had only been two shots, but within seconds, it became a beautiful symphony of automatic weapons punctuated by the occasional scream.

"Sounds like our cue," I said nervously.

"That it does. Stay close," he said, taking my hand and leading me out into the hallway.

I could see patients up and down the hallway stepping out of their rooms to investigate, but when the power suddenly went out, a lot of bodies disappeared the way they'd come. We stayed low and hugged the wall, moving fast. I had no idea where we were going, but Justice was leading the way like he'd grown up playing in these halls as a kid. Undoubtedly his attention to detail and preparation led him to study the hospital's layout in case he'd had to pull a jail break from here. Whatever the reason, I wasn't mad at him in the slightest because within moments, he had us moving fast through a side door and outside into the crisp night air. I was looking around for a SUV with his homies leaning out the windows firing shots to be our getaway vehicle, but all was quiet on this side of the building.

"Get in," he demanded, moving towards an all-black 2017 Ford Mustang.

I quickly hopped in the passenger seat while he slid behind the wheel, and seconds later we were moving. I was just about to congratulate him on a clean getaway when I heard the sound of angry bullets raining on the car's trunk. Justice immediately mashed his foot down on the gas, propelling me into the seat as the car took off like it was powered by rocket fuel.

"Put your seat belt on," he demanded, weaving through oncoming traffic as horns blared and high beams flashed in our direction. I did as I was told while watching in fascinated horror as Justice lived out his *Fast and Furious* dreams. I'd never seen him handle a car like he was right now, but it was clear that he knew what he was doing. Of course, that didn't help the decision my recently eaten hamburger was trying to make because with one turn, it was ready to come flying in chunks out of my throat, but with another, I thought I was gonna shit myself. Honestly I don't care which happened as long as we got away in one piece.

"There's a car coming up on your side," he said suddenly.

I barely had time to grab my pistol before an old school Lincoln came into view with an angry Mexican behind the wheel. For some reason it crossed my mind to wind down my window before I started shooting, but thankfully, my common sense kicked in and took over. My passenger window shattered, as I squeezed off four quick shots, and the car that had been next to me veered off into the back of a parked truck. I felt the heat from the explosion even as we drove fast away from it.

"Nice," Justice commented.

"Thanks. Duck!" I demanded, taking aim at the car outside his window and shooting until it disappeared from view.

"I guess my homies weren't exaggerating about being outnumbered."

"It has to be both cartels," I said, looking behind us to see who was still in pursuit.

I could see headlights moving up on us quick, but when I turned back around, I saw red and blue lights heading towards us.

"Good response time," I said, looking in the side mirror.

The lights that I'd seen moments before weren't there anymore, but I still wasn't about to take a deep breath until we were safely out of Texas.

"How long will it take you to get us out of the country?" I asked.

"Where are we going?"

"Dubai is nice this time of year," I replied, smiling at him.

"I've never been, but I heard that it's a good place to relocate to if you have money."

"It is, plus my dad did business over there on his own, so we should still be able to make money without fearing Ivy's interference," I said.

"Even better. It should only take about - "

I could tell by the way he slammed on the brakes that he'd seen what I did. A car had just swerved across the center line into our lane. It could've been a drunk driver, but I couldn't tell though because the headlights were blinding me, so I tightened my grip on the gun in my hand. When Justice turned the wheel to move around, that's when shit got real. The car quickly accelerated and swerved in front of us, and I saw two things that made my heart stop beating in my chest. With the car's lights no longer facing us, I got a clear look at Ivy in the passenger seat, and she was holding something gold out the window.

"Son of a bitch," Justice mumbled.

I could tell by the sound in his voice that any doubts he'd had about that bitch being alive had just went out the window. Before either of us could react, though, flames leapt from the gun in Ivy's hand, drilling two neat holes in the windshield.

"J!" I yelled, pulling him towards me, while trying to make him put his foot down on the gas pedal.

"Come on, come on, J, you gotta drive," I said, crying in despair and anger.

Even if I hadn't seen the bullets hit him squarely in the chest, I'd know he was hurt badly by his labored breathing and his lack of speech.

"Justice!" I sobbed, holding him tighter.

I tried pulling him all the way into the passenger seat so that I could get behind the wheel, but when I suddenly felt a gun barrel at the back of my head, I knew that there was no use.

"I really missed you, *sis*. Come on, spend some time with me," Ivy said sweetly.

My eyes landed on the gun a few inches from my fingers, but before I could move, I heard the hammer cock on a gun being levelled at me through the driver side window.

"I don't mind you dying right here," the Spanish guy pointing the gun at me said, smiling.

"I'm already dead," I replied softly.

Aryanna

Chapter 18
Ivy
Two days later

"What you doing, bae?" Big asked, coming into my office.

"Just going over the quarterly reports for the ports in Laredo and Galveston.

"You need any help?" he asked, flopping down in the chair across from me.

"Nah, I got it, baby.

I was looking for you earlier so that I could tell you about the meeting I had earlier with Chief Stringer."

"I'm sorry, I was with the homies trying to get everybody resettled out here. We don't want mu'fuckas stepping on each other's toes because you know I had to redistribute some territory when I sent niggas to Cali," he replied.

"You got everything straight?" I asked, glancing away from the spreadsheet on the computer screen in front of me.

"Yeah, we good, and all available bodies are searching for Ebony and Justice. What did Stringer say? Does he know where they're at?"

"The only address he has belongs to that house in Dallas, and since her ankle monitor is still working, he can't reissue a warrant to lock her back up," I replied frustrated.

"They could be in that house, but there's no way for us to know because there's no angle to sneak up on them from."

"If we would've been on top of shit the other night - "

"I know, baby, and I've apologized for that. I didn't expect to have to deal with one of the homies getting robbed and pistol whipped, but we had to hit the streets and handle that shit ASAP," he said.

"I get it. I just hate that we missed an opportunity. With them being on the run more or less, though, I met with Stringer and my lawyer Joey so we can get our stories straight about my sudden resurrection."

"Wait, what? You're going public about being alive?" he asked, clearly surprised.

"Yeah, I've got too many things to handle to be playing in the shadows. Plus, I need the FBI to disappear from our life, but if they stumbled upon the truth instead of hearing from me, they'd be worse than a dog with a bone," I replied.

"All that sounds good, but don't you think that we should've talked about this first?"

"Pull out your phone and tell me how many missed calls you have from me," I said, sitting back in my chair and looking at him.

"Don't act like that decision had to be made immediately, Ivy. You could've waited until I got home."

"Ah, so now I'm supposed to wait on you before I make business decisions, but you don't have to give me the same courtesy?" I asked.

"What the fuck are you talking about? You don't seriously expect me to call you and tell you what I'm about to do when it comes to a situation in the street, do you?"

"Is it a business decision? And doesn't the business decisions in the street affect all other avenues of business?" I asked calmly.

"Okay, but I don't need you to hold my hand."

"Likewise," I replied, smiling.

"Funny, smartass, but your decision puts you and my daughter in danger because in case you've forgotten, Justice and Ebony want your black ass dead."

"Believe me, I ain't forgot shit, and the feeling is absolutely mutual. Stop worrying, baby, I know what I'm doing," I said reassuringly.

The look he was giving me was intense, but we both knew what he was gonna say in the end. It would be emasculating to remind him that this queen really ran the kingdom, but we both knew that truth was indisputable. I knew that he could let this go, just like I knew it don't matter because all truths would be told soon.

"So now that you're back from the dead, what are your intentions?" he asked.

"Underworld domination of course."

"Ah, so does that mean you still want to take over parts of Mexico?" he asked sarcastically.

"Actually no, I'm more realistic these days. I want a firm grip on South America as a whole, and North America too, for that matter," I replied.

His laughter was instantaneous, but I didn't so much as crack a smile. It amazed me that I never noticed how limited Big's imagination was, but maybe that was because I'd never conversed with someone in this game that didn't lack vision. My dad and I never had the opportunity to chop it up about all the doors that his life's work had opened, but recently, Juanito had opened my eyes to the endless possibilities. The empire that Soloman Black built was mostly legal, and I had familiarized myself with all aspects of it since taking over. My goal now was to make sure that the empire kept growing in a way that allowed my daughter to live off the interest. I'd thought that would mean going completely legit, but Juanito had explained that it would always be better to have wolves and not need them, than to need them and not have them. Acquiring more wolves and more territory were my immediate goals.

"You're *not* serious. Ivy, we've had this conversation, and you know that you'll never be their equal."

"It seems like you're the one who ain't serious because you're still thinking that I wanna be their equal," I said, shaking my head sadly.

"Okay, so what are you saying? You're gonna run two continents?" he asked in disbelief.

"Something like that. But that comes later. For now, you might wanna get ready if you're planning to attend tonight's meeting with me."

"What meeting?" he asked, giving me a confused look.

"I called a meeting with Manuel, Juanito, and Hoover Slim. I just wanted to make sure that we're all on the same page about everything so that there are no misunderstandings."

The look on his face quickly shifted from confusion to an anger that he had to work hard to get under control.

"You-you called a meeting with my big homie and I'm the last one to know about it? What type of shit is that, Ivy?"

"Do I really need to suggest that you pull out your phone again and count the number of missed calls that you have from me?" I asked patiently.

The vein standing out on his temple told me just how pissed off he was, but he didn't say shit as he got up and left the room. I chuckled softly, going back to the spreadsheet in front of me. I'd put the conversation with Big out of my mind and I was completely absorbed in my work, but when my phone rang, I quickly answered it with a smile on my face.

"I was wondering when you'd call," I said, getting up and crossing the room to close my door.

"Really? So does that mean that you were sitting by the phone waiting on me to call?"

"No! The only reason I answered so fast is because you now have your own ringtone so I knew it was you, but I'm actually working right now," I replied.

"My own ringtone, huh? What song makes you think of me?"

I hesitated to answer that question, and I could feel the heat of embarrassment warming my cheeks. I knew that I was being foolish though because the odds were good that he wouldn't know what song I was talking about anyway.

"The title of the song is 'Jam'," I replied.

His laughter was quick, even though it was soft and deep, and as always, it created wetness in my panties.

"You're laughing because you don't know it, but if you did, then - "

"'Jam', by Kevin Gates, featuring Trey Songz, Ty Dolla $ign, and Jamie Foxx," Juanito said matter-of-factory.

The heat I'd felt in my face quickly spread throughout my bodies as a huge smile crept over my face.

"So you are familiar with that song."

"I don't know what would give you the impression that I wouldn't be up to date on good music. I'm only twenty-six, sweetheart, and I'm not out of touch with the culture that is hip hop," he said.

"I get the feeling that you're full of surprises, and I have a lot to learn about you."

"We have a lot to learn about each other," he corrected gently.

"It's a bit premature to be making those types of plans though," I said, coming out of the clouds and back down to reality.

"Not at all, because I know you're intelligent enough to know that I'm not dumb enough to give you up now that I have you."

"Oh, so you have me?" I asked, sitting down in my chair and getting comfortable.

"I apologize for sounding so presumptuous. I just know the chemistry that exists between us on multiple levels, and if you weren't interested in exploring the possibilities for where we could go, you wouldn't have let me inside."

"Maybe I simply fell weak that one time," I reasoned.

Again he laughed softly, making my body tingle.

"You're far from weak, Ms. Black, and you would never allow yourself to be perceived as such. I have no doubt that your husband's deception hurt, but that wasn't why we made love. We made love because we both wanted that, and more."

It was my turn to laugh now because he was speaking the Gospel and we both loved it. We'd talked several times since that infamous night a couple days ago, and it definitely felt like we were building a relationship despite me being sworn to another. A man in my position always had a few side bitches, so would it be wrong for me to have a nigga or two on standby to lay the pipe? Probably not, if I was that type of bitch.

"So would this be business or pleasure?" I asked.

"I think you know that it would be life, and together we'd live the best version of it."

"Hmm. I have to admit that you do make an interesting proposal, Juanito."

"I haven't proposed yet, sweetheart, but rest assured that it's coming," he replied seriously.

Suddenly the warmth I'd felt was heat that would've had the devil looking for sunblock. Not even the door to my office opening unexpectedly could wipe the grin off my face, but I knew that I needed to steer this conversation into safer waters.

"I'm sure that's not what you called to tell me, so what can I do for you, Juanito?"

"You can sit on my face the next time I see you," he replied seductively.

My burst of laughter had Big looking at me quizzically, but I purposely ignored it and gave him a thumbs up on the charcoal grey suit that he was wearing.

"You're laughing, but I still can't get over how delicious you taste," Juanito said softly.

"I'm sorry. I'll do what I can to fix that."

"You promise?" he asked seductively.

"I do. Is there anything else you need?"

I'd made sure to stand up and turn my back to Big so he wouldn't see the smile that I couldn't control.

"I'm pretty sure that your ex-husband is in the room with you right now so I won't insist that you tell me you love me. Let me ask you this though: do you want my dick inside you right now?"

"Yes," I replied truthfully.

"You didn't say it like you *really* wanted it though."

I tried to suppress my laughter, but I couldn't, and I knew that I was flirting with danger.

"I want it, Juanito, and you know that, so stop playing."

"Okay, you don't have to be so pushy. I'll see you soon," he replied, laughing as he hung up.

I could feel Big's eyes on me before I turned around, but I knew trying to avoid his stare would indicate guilt. I didn't need to feel guilty, especially not when it came to forsaking my wedding vows.

"You and Juanito are real friendly these days," Big commented.

"Yeah, I guess. Manuel is turning more of the cartel's business over to him, which means I'll be dealing with him more now."

"Since when do you have to be friends to handle business?" he asked.

"Since most people would perceive it as rude to rebuff a casual friendship between business partners. When did you become so insecure?"

"I'm not insecure. I just know that you'd be in your feelings if I had a female friend/business associate," he replied defensively.

"You mean like Star?"

To his credit, he managed to keep a straight face at the mention of her name, but I had no doubt that was only because he thought I knew less than I did. That was exactly what I wanted him to think.

"Star is the homie, meaning that I took an oath to always be there for her. You don't owe Juanito that kind of loyalty."

"Don't I though? Think about how differently all of this would've played out had it not been for the Gulf Cartel's support and loyalty." I pointed out, slipping my phone into my blazer pocket as I stepped into my red six inch heels.

"Don't mistake their loyalty for money as them being loyal to you."

"Don't worry, I'm clear on where *everybody's* loyalty lies," I replied, smiling.

The way he looked me over from head to toe would've turned me on once upon a time, but now I just felt indifferent as I smoothed out the wrinkles in my black knee length dress that matched my blazer. I grabbed my purse and made sure my gun was in it before pulling my red lipstick out, and applying a fresh coat to my mouth.

"How do I look?"

"Too damn good," he replied.

"There's no such thing. Let's go before we're late, and I'm driving."

I led the way out of the house to my red Rolls Royce and slid behind the wheel. Once Big was beside me, I started the car and we were on the move.

"Where's James and his people?" Big asked, looking behind us.

"We're good. I mean, this bitch is bulletproof, ain't it?"

"Don't be a smartass, Ivy, because you know damn well that a bulletproof car don't prevent an ambush."

"God, what the fuck happened to your sense of humor?" I said, shaking my head and speeding through the front gate.

I put on the Kevin Gates CD *Islah* and cranked the volume up to discourage any conversation from the passenger seat. I knew that he probably thought I simply didn't wanna talk to him or argue, and he was right to a certain degree, but honestly, it was deeper. Ever since that night outside of Star's house, I'd been asking myself what I was gonna do about Big "allegedly" cheating on me. I mean, we'd been together a long time, which meant that we had what it took to endure this test of our relationship. Right? That's what I'd thought until words like allegation and suspicion went out the window, and the proof of his infidelities became indisputable and undeniable. Once that happened, I was back to asking myself what I was gonna do about it, and part of me was content with continuing to act like I didn't know what he was up to. That was some weak bitch shit though, and a woman with my ambitions couldn't be on no weak bitch shit in the slightest. Every move that I made had to be one of calculation because my friends and enemies were waiting on a misstep, or hoping to discover a chink in my armor. My dad had warned me of this when he'd told me to keep my eyes on *everybody*, including Big. At the time, I'd thought he was tripping because Big would *never* hurt me, but my father had been speaking from a position of experience that he wished he'd never known. He'd wanted me to understand that if someone as close as Jacob was to him could betray him and our entire family, then who wouldn't fuck us over? I understood the last lesson that my dad had wanted to instill in me, and it hurt to learn it intimately, but at least I was still alive. So what did I do about Big? At this point, all I knew was that I'd been raised to keep my word, which meant I knew what I had to do.

"Where are we going?" Big asked an hour into our journey.

"My townhouse."

"Why'd you schedule the meeting there? You ain't been there in a minute," he said.

"It was actually Hoover Slim who suggested it because he knew it wasn't on anybody's radar. It's cool. I mean, it's not like I have another use for it now that I've moved into my parents' old house."

I thought he might have more questions, but he let it go, and we continued riding on consumed by our own individual thoughts. An hour and a half later we pulled up outside my townhouse, and judging by the amount of cars in front of my spot, we were the last ones to arrive.

"We're late," I said, annoyed.

I got out of the car and led the way inside. Juanito greeted me in the hallway with a powerful hug that took me off my feet.

"Put my wife down, nigga. Fuck you think - "

His sentence was cut short by the gun being pressed to the back of his head.

"Calm down, homie," Hoover Slim said, relieving Big of his pistol.

"What-what the fuck is this?" Big asked, putting his hands up.

"All your questions will be answered, baby. Just follow me," I said, leading the way into the dining room.

As soon as Big entered the room, I could tell that he understood in part what this was about.

"You know Starmel, don't you?" I asked, pointing at the very pregnant woman sitting at my dining room table.

Aryanna

Chapter 19
Ivy

"Bae, this is a situation that we can handle in private, after the business is attended to," Big said, looking at the other occupants seated at my dining room table.

"This *is* business that needs tending to though, bae, and it's why everyone is here," I replied.

"Sit down," Hoover Slim demanded, pushing Big towards the chair across from Star.

The look that Big gave Star was telling her to keep her mouth shut, but the one she returned summed up the theme for today. Too late. I took my seat at the head of the table with Juanito sitting at my right and Manuel sitting at my left. Hoover Slim remained standing behind Big with the barrel of his .40 Desert Eagle inches from the back of Big's head, while Star's boyfriend took a similar position with his Glock .19 pointed at Star's head.

"Gentlemen, I apologize for being late, but now that we're all here let's get down to business. Hoover Slim, you can start," I offered.

"I can't lie, this is a sad day for me because I never expected to be in this situation with one of my favorite homies. Rules are rules though. Big Cuzz, you knew that Star was Big Hog's wife, but you fucked her anyway and got her pregnant. You're in violation," Hoover Slim said, shaking his head sadly.

"That ain't my baby, and Star and I ain't been fucking!"

The look on Big's face told me that he actually believed those lies that he was kickin'. He was the only one that believed them though.

"Star," I said.

"It's-it's Big's baby. Hog can't have no kids, and Big is the only other person that I was fucking."

"That bitch is *lying*!" Big exclaimed angrily.

"No, she's not," Hog said, glaring at Big like he wanted to put a bullet in him right then.

"Star's seven months pregnant, which means that she's far enough along for a DNA test to be done. So we did one," I stated casually.

Hearing this had Big looking like a fish out of water as he opened and closed his mouth, clearly wanting to kick bullshit while realizing how useless it would be.

"What would a violation like this carry as far as punishment goes?" I asked Hoover Slim.

"Normally a vicious ass whooping, but because his actions jeopardized the safety of the organization and its business associates - "

"Whoa, hold the fuck up! Now you're just making shit up because me fucking that bitch ain't do all that," Big insisted.

"Didn't it though?" I asked, letting some of my anger come to the surface as I stared at the man I'd loved.

"Two nights ago the opportunity presented itself to handle the enemies who've posed a threat to you, your organization, and your family, but you couldn't handle it because you were fucking her," Juanito said, nodding his head in Star's direction.

"You don't know what the fuck you're talking 'bout! You're so obsessed with my wife that you'll say whatever to make me look bad."

I could tell Big was ready to leap across the table as he addressed Juanito, and the smile on Juanito's face was goading him into doing it.

"He's not making shit up against you, Big. He and I both saw your car parked outside Star's house at 1 a.m. That's why you didn't answer your phone when I called, and that's why - "

"Ebony and Justice got away. Yeah, I know. Don't act like they were coming to attack you and I wasn't there to protect you, because that wasn't what happened. I'll find them and deal with them," Big said dismissively.

"Oh, I'm already dealing with them. They never actually got away that night because Juanito and I work well together," I replied, smiling at the man sitting beside me.

"Bitch, I - "

His sentence and movements were stopped by the sounds of Hoover Slim cocking his pistol.

"Big, you cannot be mad when you so obviously made your choice," Manuel said, pointing towards the swollen belly of Star.

"You don't know what the fuck you're talking about. Ivy is my wife and that don't change simply because I stuck my dick in this bitch a few times."

"Disrespect my wife one more time," Big Hog threatened, swinging his gun in Big's direction.

"Actually, Big, you sticking your dick in any female other than me forfeited your rights as my husband. The same as if I'd allowed any man besides you to stick his dick in me."

The look that Juanito and I shared made me glad that I didn't wear panties because they would be nothing except wet silk at this point.

"Ivy, you don't mean that. We've been through too much for you to mean what you're saying right now. I'm your husband and you love me."

"Actually, you're her ex-husband because she had your marriage annulled, and she loves me," Juanito stated, smiling his beautiful smile.

As quick as an alley cat, Big was on top of the dining room table, scrambling to get to Juanito, but a well-placed bullet in the thigh halted his progress.

"Act accordingly," Manuel advised, tucking his pistol back inside his suit jacket.

"I'm gonna kill you, bitch! *Both* of you!" Bog growled, looking at me and Juanito while he clutched his leg.

Hoover Slim pulled him down off the table and back into his seat, while everyone looked on at the sad sight he'd become. I was pretty sure that being a street nigga meant that Big had envisioned his end before, but it probably never looked like this. I stood up and pulled my gun out of my purse before making my way to Big's seat.

"It's crazy that even in this moment when I have every right to hate you and despise you, I'm just like any other woman who finds herself in this position. I'm wondering why. I mean, I'm a good woman, Big. I've stood by you through any and everything, and helped you to build the future that we wanted. Why? Why cheat on me?"

"Ivy it's not that serious. I don't love her, I only love *you*, and I know that you know that. Don't let no one get in your ear and convince you of anything else because you *know* me."

I calmly put my gun to his temple.

"And you know *me,* sweetheart. I told you that I'd shoot you if you ever cheated on me, and I'm a woman of my word," I said softly, pulling the trigger.

The power of my .45 knocked him out of the chair, and the roar of it made Star jump as tears ran freely down her face.

"Star, I would *love* to put your brains on my carpet right next to your baby daddy's, but Big Hog is your husband and I think that entitles him to handle you how he sees fit," I said, reclaiming my seat at the head of the table, and sitting my gun down in front of me.

"Get up, bitch," Big Hog demanded, pulling Star out of the chair by her hair.

They left the room, leaving the rest of us to discuss the remaining business.

"I hope that this proves to you that nothing supersedes business, and that we can continue to do good business in the future," Hoover Slim said.

"We'll definitely continue our business relationship because expansion is a part of my immediate plans, which means the muscle that you provide will be appreciated. All I ask is that you make sure those that you deal with under your umbrella are those that you trust with your life," I replied.

My comment made him smile because he understood exactly what I was saying to him. I may have been green when he and I first met, but I'd never be that again, and my husband's body on the ground at his feet proved that I understood the necessity of death. When the time came, I knew that my life wouldn't be spared, nor would those that I loved. Therefore I would spare no one.

"I understand, Ivy, and I'll be doing a thorough house cleaning in the immediate future when it comes to Hoover and anyone we're affiliated with. I'll contact you when I'm ready to get back to the money."

I nodded my head in agreement and he left the room. That left myself, Juanito, and Manuel seated at my dining room table.

"That went well," Juanito said.

"It did, didn't it? Thank you both for supporting my moves," I replied genuinely.

"There's no need for thanks, Ivy. As I have told Juanito on more than one occasion, you're *absolutely* Soloman's daughter, and it shows in every decision that you make. Your father is proud of you, as am I."

I forced myself to swallow the emotions that were beating in my chest, but I couldn't help the smile that I knew was lighting up my face. The decision to kill Big hadn't been an easy one by any means, but if he was comfortable fucking around on me, then in his heart, he was already comfortable fucking me over. That type of betrayal had to be cut out quick so that the cancer didn't spread. I knew Juanito wasn't the same type of man, but I'd still be going into this situation with my eyes wide open because it was up to me to protect me.

"Have you figured out what you want to do about Ebony?" Juanito asked.

"We all know how that situation needs to end, so the only obstacle is the baby," I replied.

"I support whatever decision you make. Just keep me informed," Manuel rose, and leaned over to kiss my cheek.

Juanito got up and escorted him outside, leaving me with Big's warm body and my thoughts to keep me company. To kill Ebony's baby or not to kill Ebony's baby, that was the question. I was so deep in thought trying to tackle this issue from multiple angles that I didn't realize Juanito had returned until I felt his hands on my shoulders.

"I like the fact that you didn't jump even though I know you didn't hear me. It proves that you feel safe with me."

"Is there any reason that I shouldn't?" I asked, looking up at him.

"Of course not."

His kiss was gentle, yet thorough, and again came with a familiarity that I didn't understand. I was more than okay with it though. Before I knew it I was in his arms and he was carrying me out of the room.

"Where's your bedroom?"

I pointed in the general direction before pulling his mouth back down to mine. Moments later I felt myself being lowered to the softness of my mattress, and then I was stripped of all my clothing except my high heels. When he had me just how he wanted me he took a step back and gave me a strip tease that left my mouth dry and my pussy dripping. We'd both seen each other naked, but the difference between day and night gave us a different appreciation for this moment.

"Fuck me," I demanded, spreading my legs wide open for him.

The fact that he shook his hair free of its ponytail before climbing onto the bed with me was so sexy, and I started to tell him that, but he took my breath away by diving balls deep inside me. His first few strokes spoke to his willingness to meet my demands, but his combination of speed and long strokes made me question if I'd bit off more than I could chew. I could hear my pussy gushing over the steady knocking of the headboard against the wall.

"Juan-Ju-Juan!" I moaned, holding onto him tightly.

"I-I love you, Ivy!"

Even if I'd wanted to reply, he made that impossible by bending my legs up in a way that brought my heels together, and pounding his dick in me until it felt like he was in my stomach. I came instantly, and that only made my pussy more sensitive to his onslaught. I could feel his dick throbbing wildly, making me think that he was gonna cum, but he didn't. He fucked me savagely for fifteen minutes, making me cum again and beg for more. When he finally relinquished control, I rolled him on his back and rode him like we were in a Western.

"You-you love me?" I asked, pumping my hips faster.

"S-si! Te amo mucho, my amor!"

"Say it like-like you mean it," I demanded, twisting his nipples as I popped my pussy on him.

The beautiful Spanish that spewed from his lips was rapid and incoherent, but I felt his cum shoot up into me with the force of a shotgun blast. The dick didn't go down and I didn't stop riding him like I was trying to outrun the law. A few minutes later I came hard enough to knock the wind out of me, forcing me to collapse on his chest.

"You okay?" he asked, sucking in oxygen.

"Uh huh."

When I finally moved so that I could lay beside, him he turned on his side and pulled me towards him like we were about to spoon. I didn't have a problem with that, but suddenly I felt him grab a fistful of my hair as he pushed his dick back inside me.

"We're not done yet."

A half hour later my arms finally gave out, and I fell face first into my pillow, trembling uncontrollably.

"Y-you win," I panted, rolling over onto my back and staring at the smile on Juanito's face.

"We'll call it a d-draw."

He collapsed next to me, and this time he pulled me into his arms with the intention of holding me. I didn't want shit to be awkward between us, but I knew I was gonna have to clear the air because misunderstandings between us came with too many repercussions to take it likely.

"It feels like we're in a relationship."

"It felt like that to me when I cooked for you last week, but maybe that was simply wishful thinking on my part," he replied.

"So was this what you were wishing for?"

"No, I wished for more. So much more," he said, holding me tighter.

"Juanito, I-I need to take this slow. I was in a relationship with Big for a long time, so I'm not even sure that I knew how to be with someone else. I don't want to hurt you, or get hurt."

"I would never hurt you, Ivy, not even unintentionally. I didn't tell you that I love you because your pussy is phenomenal. I love you because you're phenomenal. I truly understand that, which meant that I'll go as slow as you need, and give you all the time that you need."

"What if I need that time without us having sex?" I asked, looking up at him.

"Okay."

If I hadn't been looking at him to see just how serious he was I'd have thought that he was full of shit.

"No matter what happens I don't want our business relationship and our friendship to get fucked up. Can you promise me that?" I asked.

"Yes, I can. I see our union as like back in the day when two ruling families would arrange a marriage of their heirs to the throne, and that would create a dynasty that would rule for centuries to come. We can do that, and we've already started on the next generation."

The way he rubbed my stomach lovingly stopped me from asking if he could see himself raising another man's baby. He could, and he would. What he said about ruling families and history had crossed my mind long before this moment because that was how a bitch ran two continents.

Juanito and I had the vision and ambition to run the world, so what was stopping us? The answer was simple. *Nothing.*

"I think I know how I want to handle the situation with Ebony's baby."

"I'm behind you no matter what," he said without hesitation.

"Promise?"

"Para siempre," he vowed.

Chapter 20
Ebony
Six months later

The moment my water broke, I went from dead sleep to wide awake like a starter pistol had been fired in my ear. The pain was enough to make it hard to breathe, but the fear swirling through my body was enough to make me believe that a panic attack was in my immediate future. From the information that I'd absorbed over the last six months I knew that almost every first time mother experienced fear that was paralyzing, but that wasn't what this was. Sure, I was scared to give birth, but I was utterly terrified about what would happen *after* I gave birth. Ivy hadn't been specific about what she intended to do with me once I had my baby, but I wasn't naïve enough to believe that we'd both continue breathing. In my last six months of imprisonment here at Ivy's parents' house, I'd gone over so many scenarios of what that bitch could be planning for me that I truly felt like I'd lost my mind! And the part that tortured me the most is that Ivy didn't give me a hint! Outside of slicing both of my Achilles tendons and shattering both of my knees to ensure that I couldn't run away, she'd done absolutely nothing to harm me or my baby. She'd made sure that I got regular care from a doctor, kept a nurse on call, and made sure that I had all the medications I needed to keep me and my baby healthy. She treated me like I was her sister, but I had no illusions about how she really felt. The fact that I was even now lying in the same bed that her dad had been in before I executed him was proof that the bitch hadn't forgotten shit, and she wanted me to know that. So even though the words hadn't been spoken, I figured that my daughter's arrival would result in one or both of us dying. My biggest fear had been that Ivy would let me have my baby only to turn around and kill her in front of me. Rockafella had died in front of me, and so had Justice, but to lose my little girl before my very eyes... If I wasn't crazy already, that would definitely push me over the edge. This knowledge coupled with the fear I felt is what had me wanting to deny the truth of what was happening right now.

A sudden contraction had me pinned to the bed, sweating, while trying to figure out what the hell I was gonna do. I needed to get the fuck out of here, but I knew that was beyond impossible. Knowing how limited my options were made my fear ratchet up a notch, and somehow that made my next contraction hit harder.

"Ivyyyy!" I yelled, unable to hold my tears back any longer.

My breathing exercises came as second nature, and thankfully, that helped reduce the pressure that was threatening to rip me in half.

"Help!" I yelled once I had enough oxygen in my lungs.

I could hear the sound of footsteps in the hallway outside my room, but none of them stopped at my door. If somebody didn't come soon, I was gonna have to try to slide my big ass into the wheelchair beside my bed and roll to a nurse.

"Somebody help!" I yelled again.

A few seconds later the light flickered on and I could see James coming towards me.

"What do you want, Ebony?"

"I need a-a doctor, I'm in labor."

"Now is not the time for that joke because - "

"Does it look like I'm fucking joking?" I asked snatching the covers back, revealing my naked torso and the puddle of liquid in the bed.

"You gotta be shitting me," he said in disbelief, shaking his head.

"Get-get the doctor!"

The arrival of another soul-gripping contraction forced me to close my eyes and pray, and by the time I opened my eyes again, I was alone. I wanted to scream my head off until a medical professional arrived with dope pure enough to rewrite Pablo Escobar's history, but the last contraction left me too weak to do anything except breathe. After a few minutes I felt strong enough to try yelling, and as soon as I opened my mouth, a familiar face came into the room.

"You finally come to finish me off, huh?"

"If I wanted you dead you would've died right next to your dude," Juanito said, moving quickly to my side.

"Well, if you're not gonna kill me, then get the doctor because my baby is coming."

"Yeah, it seems like God really has a sense of humor. The doctor is busy, but I was told to take you to him."

I didn't have time to ask questions or argue before he'd scooped me up in his arms, and we quickly left the room. I expected him to carry me outside, but instead he carried me up the stairs to the master suit. When we came into the room, my disbelief and fear about being in labor flew out the window as I took in the sight of Ivy naked, sitting in an inflatable kiddy pool full of water.

"What the fuck is this?" I asked.

"She's in labor, the doctor said calmly.

"No way," I mumbled.

"W-what are the odds," Ivy growled, clearly wrestling with a contraction.

As soon as Juanito sat me down in the warm water, my own contraction reared its ugly head, and the fight was once again on.

"W-we're really having our daughters together," I said, looking over at Ivy.

The smile that she gave me took me back to when we were kids, more specifically back to when we were thirteen and we saw our first dick. We'd experienced that together too, daring a boy named Tommy to whip it out since he talked so much shit about how big and beautiful it was. Tommy had been fifteen at the time, and he couldn't let two thirteen-year-old virgins call his bluff, so he'd taken us around the side of a building and showed us all of him.

"I wonder where-where Tommy is?" she said, reading my mind.

"I don't know, but I'd like to kick his ass because he never said that dick would get us here."

It was hard to laugh through contractions, but somehow we managed it.

"Do I even want to know what you're talking about?" Juanito asked, moving to Ivy's side and taking her hand in his.

"It's not important. All that matters is that you're here."

The fact that he'd made this seemingly genuine statement to a man who wasn't Big had a mountain of questions threatening to tumble from my mouth, but my daughter made sure my focus stayed on her.

A redheaded nurse that I'd never seen before came into the room and went straight to Ivy's side.

"How are you holding up Ivy?"

"I'm fine, Shannon, but, uh, as you can see, there's about to be more than one miracle tonight. She can use your help."

Shannon immediately moved to my side and began to coach me through my breathing exercises. I was crying once again, but now it was because I understood what Ivy had never said. I was gonna die, but instead of torturing me, beating me, or raping me, she was forcing me to live and die with the knowledge that she was better than me. She was treating me with the common decency that we both knew I didn't deserve, and that would forever haunt me. I hated Ivy right now more than I ever had, but it was purely based on the fact that I loved her still. I thought that all I'd done would free me from the love and bond that we once shared, but there really was no running from the truth in the end. In trying to destroy her, I'd destroyed myself, just like my father had done when he set these events in motion.

Throughout my labor I tried to find something, anything, to prove myself wrong, but I could no longer tell myself the lies that I'd used to make it this far. Accepting this, I focused on bringing my little girl into the world while praying that she would be better than me. After an hour in the pool, Ivy became a mom while I looked on in amazement, and two hours after that, my own bundle of joy added to the world's population. My daughter was so beautiful that it hurt my heart to stare at her, but I couldn't turn away. I was relieved that I wouldn't need a DNA test to determine who her father was - not that it mattered at this point. Despite Ivy having her baby before me, she'd remained in the pool with me, holding her baby and breastfeeding her until she went to sleep. Now I did the same thing. Everybody had cleared out of the room, leaving us and our children alone, and it felt absolutely right.

"What are you gonna name her?" Ivy asked softly.

"I was thinking about naming her Rita, if that's okay with you."

"That's funny, because I was thinking about naming my daughter Marissa."

We both chuckled softly at the irony.

"We were raised by two beautiful, strong woman, and no matter what happens, we'd want our girls to embody everything they stood for," I said honestly.

"I'll make sure they live up to their namesakes."

This declaration coming from her mouth made me look at her in silent evaluation for a few moments.

"Is my daughter gonna live past today, Ivy?"

"That depends on you, Ebony. You hold that little girl's fate in your hands."

"I'll do whatever I have to do in order to save my little girl's life," I said sincerely.

For a moment she simply stared at me, not speaking, but clearly thinking.

"Juanito," she called suddenly.

Like magic he appeared, going to her and kneeling at her side. I couldn't hear what she whispered, but he nodded his head and took little Marissa from her arms before disappearing again. He returned and held his arms out to me. I looked at Ivy and she nodded her head that it was okay.

"I love you so much baby girl. I'm sorry," I said, kissing her on her lips and forehead.

My tears blinded me, but I could still see well enough to take what Juanito handed me. No one had to explain to me what needed to be done now and even though I knew the exchange was more than fair, it still hurt my heart.

"Will you tell her about me?" I asked.

"Only if you want me to tell her the ugly truth. In my opinion, it's best that they're raised as sisters."

"I wish we could've stayed that way," I said sincerely.

"We'll always be sisters, Ebony, despite everything that happened. There's no way to rewrite our history."

I nodded my head at the truth in what she said, looking down at my hands. After taking a few deep breaths, I flipped the razor in between my fingers, put it to the vein in my wrist, and pulled it towards me swiftly. I repeated the same thing with my right wrist before letting the razor slip from my grasp, and dropping my arms into the water.

"Love her for me, Ivy, please."

"I will, I promise."

"I love you, bitch," I said, smiling weakly.

"I love you too."

The tears sliding down her face surprised me, but not as much as her pulling me into her arms. I didn't know what to say, so I didn't say anything. I laid in my best friend's arms and stared at the ceiling...until I couldn't see anything...

The End

Submission Guideline

Submit the first three chapters of your completed manuscript to ldpsubmissions@gmail.com, subject line: Your book's title. The manuscript must be in a .doc file and sent as an attachment. Document should be in Times New Roman, double spaced and in size 12 font. Also, provide your synopsis and full contact information. If sending multiple submissions, they must each be in a separate email.

Have a story but no way to send it electronically? You can still submit to LDP/Ca$h Presents. Send in the first three chapters, written or typed, of your completed manuscript to:

LDP: Submissions Dept
Po Box 870494
Mesquite, Tx 75187

DO NOT send original manuscript. Must be a duplicate.

Provide your synopsis and a cover letter containing your full contact information.

Thanks for considering LDP and Ca$h Presents.

Coming Soon from Lock Down Publications/Ca$h Presents

BOW DOWN TO MY GANGSTA

By **Ca$h**

TORN BETWEEN TWO

By **Coffee**

BLOOD STAINS OF A SHOTTA **III**

By **Jamaica**

STEADY MOBBIN **III**

By **Marcellus Allen**

BLOOD OF A BOSS **VI**

By **Askari**

LOYAL TO THE GAME **IV**

LIFE OF SIN II

By **T.J. & Jelissa**

A DOPEBOY'S PRAYER **II**

By **Eddie "Wolf" Lee**

IF LOVING YOU IS WRONG… **III**

LOVE ME EVEN WHEN IT HURTS **III**

By **Jelissa**

TRUE SAVAGE **VII**

By **Chris Green**

BLAST FOR ME **III**

DUFFLE BAG CARTEL III

By **Ghost**

ADDICTIED TO THE DRAMA **III**

By **Jamila Mathis**

Aryanna

LIPSTICK KILLAH **III**

Mimi

A HUSTLER'S DECEIT 3

KILL ZONE **II**

BAE BELONGS TO ME III

By **Aryanna**

THE COST OF LOYALTY **III**

By **Kweli**

SHE FELL IN LOVE WITH A REAL ONE **II**

By **Tamara Butler**

RENEGADE BOYS **III**

By **Meesha**

CORRUPTED BY A GANGSTA **IV**

By **Destiny Skai**

A GANGSTER'S CODE **III**

By **J-Blunt**

KING OF NEW YORK V

RISE TO POWER III

By **T.J. Edwards**

GORILLAZ IN THE BAY III

De'Kari

THE STREETS ARE CALLING II

Duquie Wilson

KINGPIN KILLAZ IV

STREET KINGS 2

Hood Rich

STEADY MOBBIN' **III**

Marcellus Allen

SINS OF A HUSTLA II

ASAD

TRIGGADALE II

Elijah R. Freeman

MARRIED TO A BOSS III

By Destiny Skai & Chris Green

KINGS OF THE GAME II

Playa Ray

Aryanna

LOYAL TO THE GAME

LOYAL TO THE GAME II

LOYAL TO THE GAME III

LIFE OF SIN

By **TJ & Jelissa**

BLOODY COMMAS I & II

SKI MASK CARTEL I II & III

KING OF NEW YORK I II,III IV

RISE TO POWER I II

By **T.J. Edwards**

IF LOVING HIM IS WRONG…I & II

LOVE ME EVEN WHEN IT HURTS I II

By **Jelissa**

WHEN THE STREETS CLAP BACK I & II III

By **Jibril Williams**

A DISTINGUISHED THUG STOLE MY HEART I II & III

LOVE SHOULDN'T HURT I II III

RENEGADE BOYS I & II

By **Meesha**

A GANGSTER'S CODE I &, II III

By J-Blunt

PUSH IT TO THE LIMIT

By **Bre' Hayes**

BLOOD OF A BOSS **I, II, III, IV, V**

By **Askari**

THE STREETS BLEED MURDER **I, II & III**

THE HEART OF A GANGSTA I II& III

By **Jerry Jackson**

<u>CUM FOR ME</u>

<u>CUM FOR ME 2</u>

<u>CUM FOR ME 3</u>

<u>CUM FOR ME 4</u>

An **LDP Erotica Collaboration**

<u>BRIDE OF A HUSTLA **I II & II**</u>

<u>THE FETTI GIRLS **I, II& III**</u>

<u>CORRUPTED BY A GANGSTA I, II & III</u>

By **Destiny Skai**

<u>WHEN A GOOD GIRL GOES BAD</u>

By **Adrienne**

<u>THE COST OF LOYALTY</u>

By Kweli

<u>A GANGSTER'S REVENGE **I II III & IV**</u>

<u>THE BOSS MAN'S DAUGHTERS</u>

<u>THE BOSS MAN'S DAUGHTERS II</u>

<u>THE BOSSMAN'S DAUGHTERS III</u>

<u>THE BOSSMAN'S DAUGHTERS IV</u>

<u>THE BOSS MAN'S DAUGHTERS **V**</u>

<u>A SAVAGE LOVE **I & II**</u>

<u>BAE BELONGS TO ME I II</u>

<u>A HUSTLER'S DECEIT I, II, III</u>

<u>WHAT BAD BITCHES DO I, II, III</u>

By **Aryanna**

<u>A KINGPIN'S AMBITON</u>

<u>A KINGPIN'S AMBITION **II**</u>

I MURDER FOR THE DOUGH

By **Ambitious**

TRUE SAVAGE

TRUE SAVAGE II

TRUE SAVAGE **III**

TRUE SAVAGE **IV**

TRUE SAVAGE **V**

TRUE SAVAGE **VI**

By **Chris Green**

A DOPEBOY'S PRAYER

By **Eddie "Wolf" Lee**

THE KING CARTEL **I, II & III**

By **Frank Gresham**

THESE NIGGAS AIN'T LOYAL **I, II & III**

By **Nikki Tee**

GANGSTA SHYT **I II &III**

By **CATO**

THE ULTIMATE BETRAYAL

By **Phoenix**

BOSS'N UP **I , II & III**

By **Royal Nicole**

I LOVE YOU TO DEATH

By Destiny J

I RIDE FOR MY HITTA

I STILL RIDE FOR MY HITTA

By **Misty Holt**

LOVE & CHASIN' PAPER

By **Qay Crockett**

TO DIE IN VAIN

SINS OF A HUSTLA

By **ASAD**

BROOKLYN HUSTLAZ

By **Boogsy Morina**

BROOKLYN ON LOCK I & II

By **Sonovia**

GANGSTA CITY

By **Teddy Duke**

A DRUG KING AND HIS DIAMOND I & II III

A DOPEMAN'S RICHES

HER MAN, MINE'S TOO I, II

CASH MONEY HO'S

By Nicole Goosby

TRAPHOUSE KING **I II & III**

KINGPIN KILLAZ I II III

STREET KINGS

By **Hood Rich**

LIPSTICK KILLAH **I, II**

CRIME OF PASSION I & II

By **Mimi**

STEADY MOBBN' **I, II**

By **Marcellus Allen**

WHO SHOT YA **I, II**

Renta

GORILLAZ IN THE BAY **I II**

DE'KARI

<u>TRIGGADALE</u>

Elijah R. Freeman

<u>GOD BLESS THE TRAPPERS I, II, III</u>

<u>THESE SCANDALOUS STREETS I, II, III</u>

<u>FEAR MY GANGSTA I, II, III</u>

<u>THESE STREETS DON'T LOVE NOBODY I, II</u>

<u>BURY ME A G I, II, III, IV, V</u>

<u>A GANGSTA'S EMPIRE I, II, III</u>

Tranay Adams

<u>THE STREETS ARE CALLING</u>

Duquie Wilson

<u>MARRIED TO A BOSS... I II</u>

By Destiny Skai & Chris Green

<u>KINGS OF THE GAME II</u>

Playa Ray

BOOKS BY LDP'S CEO, CA$H

TRUST IN NO MAN

TRUST IN NO MAN 2

TRUST IN NO MAN 3

BONDED BY BLOOD

SHORTY GOT A THUG

THUGS CRY

THUGS CRY 2

THUGS CRY 3

TRUST NO BITCH

TRUST NO BITCH 2

TRUST NO BITCH 3

TIL MY CASKET DROPS

RESTRAINING ORDER

RESTRAINING ORDER 2

IN LOVE WITH A CONVICT

Coming Soon

BONDED BY BLOOD 2

BOW DOWN TO MY GANGSTA

Aryanna